By the same author

Run, Zan, Run
Missing
Bad Company
Dark Waters
Fighting Back
Another Me
Underworld
Roxy's Baby

CATHERINE MACPHAIL

WORSE THAN BOYS

BLOOMSBURY

First published in Great Britain in 2007 by Bloomsbury Publishing Plc
36 Soho Square, London, W1D 3QY

A CIP catalogue record of this book is available from the British Library

ISBN 978 0 7475 8276 2

All papers used by Bloomsbury Publishing are natural, recyclable products made
from wood grown in well-managed forests. The manufacturing processes conform
to the environmental regulations of the country of origin.

Typeset by Dorchester Typesetting Group Ltd
Printed in Great Britain by Clays Ltd, St Ives Plc

1 3 5 7 9 10 8 6 4 2

www.bloomsbury.com
www.macphailbooks.com

I loved how we walked, pushing our way across the playground, opening up paths before us while everyone watched with envy in their eyes. I could imagine us in slow motion, like in a movie, floating through the crowd, our hair flowing around us.

We were queens.

We were the best.

And I was the worst of them. Hannah Driscoll.

How did it all go so wrong?

PART ONE

THE LIP GLOSS GIRLS

CHAPTER ONE

We had been to the pictures that night and were taking the late train home. We lived at the far end of town. *They* lived on one of the worst estates in the east end. The only thing we had in common was school, Cameron High.

I spotted them first. Two carriages up from ours, four of them sitting together.

I nudged Erin, and she followed my gaze to where they sat. We would have heard them anyway, with their loud laughing and their swearing. They were always too loud. Mingers, every one of them. Scum. Call them that and they revelled in it, as if it was a compliment. The Hell Cats was what they called themselves. Hell Cats! Just showed how stupid they were that they had to give themselves a name like that.

We didn't call ourselves anything. Giving your gang a name was for daft boys or idiot girls, not for us.

But the Hell Cats had christened us the Lip Gloss Girls and the name stuck. We didn't mind. The name meant we were clean and shiny and female, but we were still the best fighters in the school.

'They get off two stops from here,' Erin said, and Heather looked up from her movie magazine.

'Who's they?' she asked.

She didn't need an answer. She knew who we were talking about. She slipped the magazine into her bag. 'How many?'

I looked down the train. I could see Wizzie. Wizzie! Wherever did she get a name like that? Tossing her black hair streaked with red, red like blood, and waving her long black-nailed fingers about. Tiny and tough, Wizzie was the scariest of them, or tried to be, always in trouble. She had her ears pierced and her nose too. She even had her eyebrow pierced. Her arms and neck were razor scarred. The rumour was she carried a knife around with her. There were three others. Lauren Winters, whose hair looked as if it had been cut by a blind barber, Sonya Taylor, the one with the stutter – and how we loved taking the mickey out of her – and big Grace Morgan, who closely resembled a horse.

We were missing our mate, Rose, that night. It was

her dad's weekend and he had taken her out for a meal.

Four of them, three of us. Still no contest.

Sonya was the first to notice us. She leant across to Wizzie and whispered and they both turned to look at us. A slow smile spread across Wizzie's face. Did she expect us to be afraid? I felt my heart beat faster and my palms began to sweat. But I wasn't afraid. I was never afraid with my mates around me. I bet none of the rest were either.

I clocked the other people in the carriage. An elderly woman reading a murder mystery, a couple of house-wives laden with shopping bags and looking as if they were desperate for a cigarette, and a man in a pinstriped business suit talking loudly on his mobile.

None of them were bothering with us.

Wizzie came through first – Wizzie always came first – swaggering up the carriage, her eyes never leaving mine. Did she think for a minute I would look away? Think again, Wizzie. I sensed Erin tense beside me. Heather just sat as if she wasn't even interested. Cool.

Wizzie burst into the carriage and suddenly every one of the other passengers took notice. The old woman, the housewives, even the man on his mobile phone – they all looked up at her.

'Typical!' Wizzie's voice was a common drawl. 'I thought you'd be hiding in the last carriage.'

I stood up too. 'Typical,' I repeated. 'Trust you not to notice us until it's your stop.'

Wizzie didn't waste any more time talking. She sprang at me, grabbing for my hair. I fell back, but I had been ready for her and my hands found her hair first. I yanked, and Wizzie let out a scream of anger. I could see Erin tackling Grace, and Heather already had Lauren and Sonya on top of her.

'You lot don't know what a fair fight is, do you?!' I yelled, and tried to claw at Wizzie's face. We both toppled to the floor. My back cracked against a seat as we fell.

The old woman was on her feet. 'Enough!' she was screaming.

The man and the two housewives didn't get up. It was the old woman who walloped at Erin with her book. Wizzie was on top of me, her fist raised, ready to smash it against my face. I felt the train begin to shudder as it pulled into the station. Their stop. The old woman dragged Wizzie off me. Wizzie kept hold of my hair, yanking me painfully up with her.

'This isn't finished.' She spoke the words so close to

my face I could feel her hot breath.

'You better believe it,' I hissed back.

The carriage doors slid open and Wizzie was on her feet and shrugging off the old woman's hand. Her foot crunched on my arm as she stepped over me. The other three followed behind her, pushing us roughly into our seats.

Once they were out, we jumped to the windows and started making faces and laughing at them. The doors slid closed again and they started shouting their abuse back at us. We pressed our faces against the window. Lauren threw the first stone, hurling it against the window. We jumped back, expecting it to shatter. It didn't, and Wizzie lifted an even bigger stone and threw it. We danced in delight as the stone glanced off the glass. They ran alongside the train as it moved off slowly, banging on the windows with their fists. If this had been a manned station someone would have stopped them. But there was nobody here. A quiet little station in the middle of a run-down, rat-infested estate.

I ran to the doors. The train was picking up speed, but the Hell Cats were still keeping up, and getting madder by the minute. I was vaguely aware of the two women and the man moving off, muttering their way into the next carriage. I grabbed the handrails and swung myself up and, with all the force I could muster, I kicked both feet against the doors. The carriage shuddered. Wizzie was so taken aback she stumbled and fell back on to the platform.

We roared with laughter as her mates gathered round to help her up.

Only the old woman was left in the carriage with us. She looked at us as if we were dirt.

'You're worse than boys!' she snapped. 'Worse than boys!'

Worse than boys. Of course we were. And that made us really laugh.

It was a good night. The best.

I thought then, how could it ever change?

CHAPTER TWO

The old bat complained about us. Can you believe that?! She was on the phone first thing on Monday morning. She recognised Wizzie. Let's face it, once you see her it's hard to forget her. That hair alone makes her stand out. And she was still in her school blazer. Between you and me, it's all she can afford to wear.

We knew something was happening when Wizzie and co were ordered from the class and practically frogmarched to the Head's office. We waited for our turn. It wasn't the first time we'd been in trouble with them. It didn't come.

I found out why just before lunchtime. Wizzie grabbed me in the corridor. She would have had me by the hair if I hadn't leapt away from her.

'What's your problem?' I yelled at her.

'We got the blame for that! Just us!' Wizzie's voice was so common. She couldn't hide her roots – not in her hair or her voice. We all made fun of the way she talked. 'You'll pay for that, pal.'

'Make us,' I said, egging her on.

Lauren jumped in, always the first to follow her leader. 'You were on that train as well. You caused as much trouble as we did. But it's always us that gets it, never the Lip Gloss Girls.'

They were gathered round me now, like zombies ready to strike. Come to think of it, that's a pretty good description of Wizzie, with her white face and that stand-to-attention hair. A zombie. But I wasn't scared. I pushed Wizzie aside. 'Your problem, not ours.'

Wizzie tried to trip me. She stuck out her foot, but at the last minute I jumped and it was Wizzie who stumbled.

'Muppet!' I shouted. And I hurried off, not running – I never ran away. There would have to be two moons in the sky before I'd run away. I just hurried as if I was trying to get away from a bad smell. I knew they hated it that I wasn't afraid of them. Even when I was on my own, I was never afraid of them. Why should I be? I had my friends to rely on, and my friends had never let me down.

Other people did, always had. My dad, leaving us

when I was only a baby. And my mum, always so bitter about men, about life, about everything. She always thought she was the one who'd been handed the sticky end of the lollipop of life.

'Nothing ever goes right for me,' was her favourite saying. 'If I didn't have bad luck I would have no luck at all. You'll be just like me, Hannah. Wait and see. Nothing ever goes right for people like us.'

But I would never be 'people like us'. I would never be like Mum, I promised myself. I was always going to be lucky. I would make things go right for me. I was going to be the best. And with friends like Erin and Heather and Rose, what could go wrong?

I told them all at lunchtime in the canteen about Wizzie. 'They must have got hell for what happened on the train, bringing down the reputation of the school and all that.'

According to the teachers, the Hell Cats were always bringing down the reputation of the school. Wearing their skirts too short, dyeing their hair, chewing gum. Common as muck.

'He probably thinks they had something to do with that mugging anyway,' Erin said.

Just a few days before an old woman had been held

17

up by a gang of girls and her pension had been stolen. It had happened on their estate, and one of the girls had threatened the old woman with a knife, so naturally, for us, Wizzie was the prime suspect.

'I love it when they get the blame!' Erin said, laughing.

'At least they didn't tell him we were there as well,' Heather said.

Erin looked at her as if she had two heads, and I could see Heather didn't like that. But honestly, sometimes Heather was so dim. I sometimes think her lift didn't go to the top floor.

'Of course they didn't,' Erin said patiently, as if she was talking to an idiot. 'That's the worst thing you could ever do. Grass on somebody, even your worst enemy.'

'We wouldn't grass on them either, Heather,' I told her.

'Wouldn't we?' She still didn't get it.

'No. But we'd get them back for it later.'

'And that's what they'll do?'

I sometimes forgot that Heather hadn't been in primary school with me and Erin and Rose. She had only become friends with us when we'd all come up to

Cameron High. She was new to our crowd, new to the Lip Gloss Girls.

I admit I preferred to think of us as the Lip Gloss Girls, because when we weren't called that, we were usually just known as Erin's crowd, and I knew even then I didn't like that. I would have liked everyone to think of us as Hannah's crowd instead.

It was Erin who answered Heather's question. 'They'll be planning their revenge already,' she said. 'So just watch your back.'

Zak Riley passed by then. I think he'd been listening all along. Zak was in our class, always winding us up. He had a mop of dark hair and he thought he was cool. Zak would never be in any gang. He thought gangs were stupid. 'You lot are unbelievable. Lassies fighting. Honestly. Will you never grow up?'

He had a cheek. He was short, with bags of attitude and one of those faces you just want to punch.

'I mean, come on, girls. Peace on earth starts here. You lot just want to fight. It's boys that are supposed to do all the fighting.' He looked at me. 'Hey, Hannah, have you ever been mistaken for a boy?'

'No,' I said at once. 'Have you?'

That sent my friends into a fit of the giggles.

Zak always got my back up. He was mouthy and lived on the same dark estate at the edge of town where Wizzie lived. He would fit in well in Wizzie's world. I looked round at his nerdy friends. 'I know we could beat you with our hands tied behind our backs.'

'You wouldn't need to do that,' Zak went on. 'One look at your face would be enough to send me running back to my mammy.'

I'd had enough of talking to him. 'Just tell your girl-friend, Wizzie, we'll be watching out for her from now on.'

He turned to his pals. 'Wizzie, my girlfriend! Ha! I'd rather kiss a tarantula.'

Zak always had a crowd of friends gathered round him, ready to laugh at his feeble jokes.

'That wee guy really annoys me,' I said as they moved off.

But we soon forgot about Zak Riley and Wizzie and any trouble that was coming. There were too many other things on our minds.

Erin's sister, Avril, was getting married and we had all been invited to the wedding. Something wonderful to look forward to and much more exciting than anything else.

CHAPTER THREE

We all gathered at Erin's house that night to admire her in her bridesmaid's dress. Erin lived in a tenement block just a few streets away from me – a roomy flat with ornate cornices on the high ceilings, and polished ceramic tiles lining the entrance close. I lived in a tenement block too, but not half so classy as Erin's.

Her dress was the colour of burnt gold, and as she posed in front of the mirror with the bedside lamps shining on her strawberry blonde hair she looked to me like some kind of sun princess.

'You suit that colour so well,' I told her.

She twirled and the colour seemed to shimmer around her. Erin's hair had glints of gold in it, anyway. No mousey brown for Erin. There was nothing mousey about Erin Brodie. She glowed.

Heather jumped up and started twirling beside her. 'This is the first real wedding I've ever been to. My sister went to the Bahamas to get married and nobody could afford to go. I think that's why she went. She doesn't like any of us.'

We all laughed. It seemed we all had family problems. Rose's mum and dad had split up and she spent her time between both of them. Though she seemed quite happy with the arrangement. 'They're both trying to win me round to their side. I get presents all the time. It's great.'

Erin was the only one of us who seemed to have the perfect family. Her mum and dad were always hugging and kissing each other, her two sisters, her brother or anyone else who was close by. Erin was the adored youngest child. The whole family doted on her. Her mother hovered around us when we were in her house. In fact, her mother was a mother hen to all of us. I thought Erin's mum was great. She was always boosting her children up, telling them how clever they were, how pretty, how well they had done. Maybe that was why they all seemed so sure of themselves.

No wonder, I thought, Erin never wanted to sleep over with any of us. She always had such fun at home. 'Mum would miss me if I stayed over with any of you,' she would say whenever we would suggest a sleepover.

And none of us ever stayed with her either. With three sisters and her brother in the house there was no room for guests. Rose never asked. Heather would have loved to have stayed over with her. I felt she hero-worshipped Erin a bit too much. But it never happened.

And me? Mum would only have moaned. Not that she would have missed me, but I could just hear her: 'Oh yes, just go and leave me on my own. I've always been on my own anyway.' She always made me feel guilty that I'd want any life away from her.

'I'm wearing my pink dress,' Heather babbled on. 'You know, the one with the shoestring straps? I'm going to look like a babe.'

'Babe was a pig, wasn't she?' I said, and Heather giggled and jumped on me, and we both fell back on the bed, laughing.

'You'll look like a pig when I'm finished with you,' she said.

We rolled on to the floor, and it was funny at first. But Heather never knew when to stop. She ruffled my hair, pulled at it, tickling me all the time. I hated that I couldn't stop laughing, as if I was enjoying myself. As if I didn't want her to stop.

Finally, I managed to push her off me, angry now.

She fell back, annoyed at me. 'Look who can't take a joke,' she said.

'You just get on my wick at times, Heather.' I stood up, feeling stupid, and I hate feeling like that.

Erin put her arm round my shoulders. 'She wouldn't dare do that to Rose.'

Heather's frown suddenly turned to a grin. 'You're right. Rose with her hair a mess, with a broken nail. "I'll die, I'll just die!"'

'I keep my nails long so I can drag them down Wizzie's face.' Rose drew her nails down Erin's radiator, and we all shivered at the sound. Anyway, Rose was used to us going on about her vanity. She thought she was gorgeous, with her thick dark curls and her violet eyes. 'I'm the one who's going to be the babe at this wedding. You wait and see.'

Heather giggled. She'd forgotten my bad temper already. I sometimes wondered if she suffered from short-term memory loss. 'I wish big Anil was going. I really fancy him.'

Anil Gupta, the best-looking boy in the school. Drop-dead gorgeous. Just about every girl fancied him, but not half as much as he fancied himself. 'As if he's going to look at any of us,' I said. 'Not when there's a mirror nearby.'

'There'll be other boys at the wedding,' Erin said. 'My brother's pals are all going. They're a lot older than we are though. I think they're more likely to be after the three other bridesmaids.'

Erin changed out of her dress and when she was back in her jeans her mum came in with cheese toasties and tea for us all and we sat on the floor and got stuck in.

As soon as her mother had gone, Erin said, 'Come on, let's play Light as a Feather.'

Our wish game. One of our favourites. Erin locked the door because her mother didn't approve – she thought it had a touch of the supernatural about it – then Erin came back and sat with us.

Everyone said you needed at least six people to play Light as a Feather, but we always did it with just the four of us. And it always worked. We were sure that was because we were special. The magic was in us.

First the atmosphere had to be captured. The room had to be dark and eerie. It really helped that the wind had got up and we could hear it whistling through the telephone cables on the street outside. We switched off all the lights except for a dim night light Erin kept by the side of her bed. And then we started to tell ghost stories. You always had to start Light as a Feather with the ghost stories.

We let Rose tell hers first. That was because her stories were always rubbish, lifted word for word or scene by scene from some horror movie she'd seen on DVD. Then it was Heather's turn. Heather couldn't tell a story to save her life. She told us the Monkey's Paw, one of the creepiest stories ever, and told us the end of the story first. She always did that.

It was Erin and I who knew how to tell a ghost story.

Erin kept her voice mysteriously soft. Her story was all about the ghost of a little girl who comes back to haunt the man who killed her. He sees her one dark night in his car mirror, sitting in the back seat, just staring at him. He looks into the back seat and she's not there. There's nothing there. But when he turns and looks into the mirror again, her face is so close, as if she's right at his shoulder, and he screams and loses control of the car. It tumbles down a ravine. And as it bursts into flame, someone sees the little girl standing on the road, looking down and smiling. She'd had her revenge. It made the hairs on the back of my neck stand up, and we all moved closer into the circle together.

Then it was my turn.

CHAPTER FOUR

I knew some great stories and made up lots more. And I always told the story as if it had really happened to me. That was my special trick.

'It was when I had the part-time job in the video shop, remember?' I knew they all could. Bruno, the owner, knew my mum and he had given me a pocket-money job, tidying up the shelves. I had only lasted a few weeks, because I never did tidy any shelves. All I did was watch videos. Bruno had given me my money one night and told me not to come back.

'I told you I was fired,' I said softly, 'but that wasn't the truth. The last night I worked there, something terrible happened.'

'Is this a wind-up? Did this really happen?' Heather was shushed by the others.

'Bruno had gone out to deliver some videos and DVDs people had rented, so I was left alone in the shop. Mary Brown was due to come in. You remember Mary Brown?'

They all nodded. Mary Brown really had worked in the video shop.

'She had lovely long blonde hair, didn't she?' Rose said.

'All of a sudden the big screen on the wall flashed into life. I hadn't switched it on or anything. It gave me a scare, but I thought Bruno must have had it on a timer. There were no customers, so I just settled down behind the counter to watch the film that was playing. Right away I thought there was something funny about it. There were no opening credits, no voiceover, just a man in a long cloak with the hood pulled low to hide his face. He was striding across some railway tracks. At first he seemed to be in the middle of nowhere, until I saw he was heading towards a shack on the edge of a town. There was no music, just the wind whining through the telegraph wires, but that only made it scarier, because I could hear the wind whistling outside the video shop too.'

We jumped as the wind suddenly got up and howled outside.

'Just like that,' I whispered. 'It was giving me the

creeps, because the video shop is pretty remote as well. I tried to turn the film off, but I couldn't find the switch. And all the time that man just kept moving nearer and nearer the shack. And I knew something awful was going to happen. He was coming for someone. Finally, I couldn't take any more and I stood outside the front door just to get away from it, but it didn't make me feel any better. That video shop is right on the edge of that big estate, it's totally isolated. I could see the lights of the houses on the other side of the football pitch, but they seemed a million miles away. There wasn't a soul about. And it was such a wild night. It was eerie standing out there too. So I went back inside. I tried not to look at the screen, but I couldn't help it. And I saw he was almost at the shack.'

Rose caught her breath. 'Wait a minute, Hannah. That video shop is right beside the railway lines . . . on the edge of town.'

I nodded. 'I know. I began to think he was coming for me. I tried to tell myself how stupid that was, it was only a film. But by then, I couldn't take my eyes off the screen. He reached the shack. He was at the back door. He began to turn the handle . . .' I held my breath, paused for just long enough to keep them in suspense.

'And right at that second I heard the back door of the video shop begin to creak open.'

Their eyes were wide. I had them.

'I screamed. I ran outside. I wasn't waiting there to see who he was or what he wanted. And I ran right into Mary, coming into work. She grabbed me and I told her what had happened.'

'What did she do?' Heather asked.

'She laughed. Said it was only a daft picture on a screen. She told me to wait there and she would go in and switch it off.'

'And did she?'

I shook my head. 'I don't know. Because Mary didn't come back out again. I shouted and shouted, but there was no answer. I was sure she was winding me up, but I was too scared to go back inside. I was so glad when Bruno arrived in his car. I told him the whole story and we both went inside. You know Bruno, he kept going on about daft lassies. He was going to fire both of us.'

Heather gasped. 'And was Mary there, lying in a pool of blood, an axe sticking out of her head?' I sometimes thought Heather had a better imagination than me!

'No.' I kept my voice soft. 'There was nobody there. The back door was wide open and Mary was gone.

Bruno was raging because Mary had left the shop unattended. He went out to check and do you know what . . . ?'

'What?'

'When I looked up at the screen on the wall. The film was still running, only this time the man was striding back over the tracks. He was carrying a girl, her long blonde hair trailing on the ground.'

Heather gasped. 'Just like Mary Brown's!'

'I know,' I said. 'I screamed when I saw it, and Bruno came running back. I pointed to the film, told him that was Mary the man was carrying, I was sure of it. And do you know what he said? He told me not to be so stupid. Mary had probably gone off with one of her boyfriends. She was always doing that. He said that was her fired for leaving the shop unattended. Then he just switched the film off. And the screen went black.'

I sat back. 'Did you like it?'

'How much of that is true?' Rose asked.

'Well,' I said in my most mysterious voice. 'No one's seen Mary Brown since that night. They all say she did run off with one of her boyfriends . . . but I think different.'

CHAPTER FIVE

The ghost stories set up the atmosphere. Now, it was time to play Light as a Feather. You must have played Light as a Feather, but in case you don't know it, I'll tell you how it works. Someone lies on the floor, like a corpse, arms folded and crossed over their chest. They have to lie silent and still, hardly breathing.

Rose wanted to be the corpse. She lay down and closed her eyes, and began to breathe deeply. I sat at her head with my hands placed gently under her shoulders, palms up. Erin and Heather took their places on either side of her. They placed their hands under her back and under her legs. In the dimly lit room I began to say softly, 'Light as a feather. Light as a feather.'

Erin and Heather took up the chant. 'Light as a feather. Light as a feather.'

Over and over again we repeated the words, almost like a litany. Softly at first, then our voices grew louder, until they became more of a demand. 'Light as a feather! Light as a feather!'

And Rose began to rise under our hands.

I don't know how it happened. I never could understand how it happened. To us it was magic. Our magic. Was there a logical explanation how we could make one of us rise? I don't know. But it amazed us every time.

I held my breath, the words now once again a whisper, a whisper of wonder. '*Light as a feather.*'

Rose lay still, her eyes closed, totally under our control as she rose up into the air.

Magic! I thought. It was magic, just like us. We were magic too.

Why couldn't things be magic like that at home? As soon as I walked through the door that night, my magic mood changed. My mum was waiting for me, eager for all the news about the wedding. She was even more excited than I was about being invited. She was in awe of Erin's family, her mother especially. That always embarrassed me so much.

'You'll have to get a really good gift. Erin's mother will expect quality.'

'Mum, we're putting money together and getting a

gift between us, I told you that.'

She shook her head. 'No. Let the others do that. You get a really good gift and it will be from you and me. I want Erin Brodie's mother to see I know how to choose quality too.'

Why did she always have to be like that? Turning even the most enjoyable occasion into a competition. She was so chuffed that Erin was my friend. Had hoped that she might be invited to the wedding too. But no one invited my mum anywhere. And I knew why.

I went to sleep that night and pushed my annoyance at Mum aside. It didn't matter. Life was so good. And if Wizzie and her mates were out to get us, that only made it better. Because we'd win.

I knew we would always win in the end.

CHAPTER SIX

I came across Sonya in the toilets next day. Or 'S-s-ssonya', as we liked to call her. I knew that was cruel, and I wouldn't have done it to anyone else who stuttered. But Sonya didn't seem to care. I was sure she only stuttered to wind us up.

I saw her eyes dart to me as I pushed my way through the door, checking to see if my mates were with me. A look of relief flashed across her face when she saw I was alone. Sonya was overweight. Not quite fat, but heading that way. I used to say they could use her for a battering ram. She didn't like that. Sonya had a reputation as a good fighter, but I'd never really seen her fight, just land on people. Honestly, that's not fighting, is it?

She sneered at me. 'You've g-got it coming, know that?'

'S-s-ssorry, S-s-ssonya, did you s-ssay s-ssomething?' Then I laughed.

Sonya's face went brick red. She threw a punch at me, but I stepped away from it, missing it easily.

'G-g-ggot to be qu-quicker than that, S-s-ssonya.'

She would have lunged at me again, but right at that moment the toilets were invaded by a bunch of older girls, prefects, always ready to step in and stop any trouble.

'What's going on here?' one of them asked.

I shrugged my shoulders. Sonya's face was red with anger. It gave her away big time. She pushed past them and crashed out of the toilets.

'You lot are always causing trouble,' Pam Ward said. Head girl, a force to be reckoned with.

I was all innocence. 'They're the ones who cause the trouble. I was only sticking up for myself.'

She didn't look as if she believed me. I didn't care. It would make a great story when I told it to the girls later on.

'You're in Erin's crowd, aren't you?' Pam said.

Why did they always say that? Just once I wanted Erin to be in my crowd, but pointing that out seemed like some kind of betrayal, so I said nothing to correct her. 'Erin's my best friend,' I said.

Pam sniggered. 'Do the other two know that?'

I pushed my way out the door, half expecting Sonya to be lying in wait for me. But it was Heather who was there. 'I heard that,' she said. 'Thanks very much. Erin's your best friend, is she? Not me.'

I put my arm around her shoulder. 'I only said that because they were talking about Erin.'

But it was a lie. Erin *was* my best friend. She and I were special. Soul mates, me and Erin. I tried to make it up to Heather as we walked to class.

There was a crowd round the school noticeboard and we pushed our way to the front. 'Hey, look what they're putting on for the school summer show! *Grease!*'

Everyone loved the school summer show, except maybe Wizzie and her lot. People like her, the low lifes, wouldn't have anything to do with the school show. But we loved it. It was always such a laugh.

'We must tell Rose. She'd be brilliant playing Sandy.' Rose was a really good singer. She had dreams of going on the stage one day. She'd been in the show the year before. She'd definitely be up for this one too.

Suddenly, Heather burst into song. '*Summer lovin', I came in last . . .*'

I joined in, totally off-key. Didn't know the words either. '*Summer lovin' . . . Wizzie got gassed . . .*'

We laughed ourselves silly as we walked up the corridor, hurrying to tell Rose about the auditions. Erin caught up with us and joined in. I noticed Sonya and Lauren watching us. Surely it was envy I saw in their eyes. What else could it be? Who wouldn't want to be •one of us?

CHAPTER SEVEN

There was a fight coming. We could all sense it. Nothing was said, but the tension was there. And it was coming from Wizzie's crowd, the Hell Cats. I said it was probably BO and we all laughed.

Even the teachers sensed it.

Mr Hammond, the teacher who produced the school show, called us together one day and asked us just what was going on.

'Nothing, Mr Hammond,' Erin said, before I had a chance to speak. She looked round at us. 'We don't know what you mean.'

Heather looked blank. Not a difficult thing for Heather. Rose just looked bored.

Mr Hammond spoke directly to Erin. 'Don't think if there's any trouble you won't get the blame. Just because you lot manage to avoid it most of the time.' He was one of the few teachers who didn't give us any slack. He thought we were every bit as much to blame for trouble as the Hell Cats. 'You think because you live in a better area you must be better than they are. Actually, that's what makes you worse.'

We all looked at each other as if he was talking Chinese.

'What are we supposed to have done wrong?' I managed to get his attention at last. He turned to me.

'You were on that train too. Don't think I don't know it. And I know how it works, Hannah. They got the blame, so Wizzie will get back at you for it. I know Wizzie and I know you lot. And you're all trouble. Not one of you any better than the other.'

'We keep back from trouble, sir. You ask anybody.' I was all wide-eyed innocence. I could see that was really annoying him.

As he finally stomped away from us, I whispered to Erin, 'But if trouble comes to us, we don't turn our back on it.'

And trouble was coming. But when? I didn't feel scared thinking about it. It was more like excitement I felt. Every time I passed Wizzie or her mates in the corridors I tensed, expecting them to lunge at me, expecting a fight at any moment. I even imagined it happening. And I'd win. Then I'd go back to Erin and tell her. 'Sorted.' I'd sorted it. Me. Hannah. I wanted to be the one who sorted everything.

I walked into the canteen and there they were, at their table. Wizzie was lying along it on her belly Lauren and Sonya were sitting on it. Big Grace had her feet resting on it. Why couldn't they ever just sit at a table like normal people? I wondered.

I decided I wasn't going to wait for them to come to me. I barged up to them instead. 'That's very un-hygienic,' I said, pointing out Wizzie's bare midriff. I noticed she'd had her belly button pierced. It had a ring attached to it. Even more unhygienic. 'Especially since it's your belly that's on the table.'

Wizzie sat up. Did she have a fresh scar on her neck? Red raw, I was sure she did.

'Cut yourself shaving?' I asked.

It was Sonya who leapt at me. Wizzie held her back. 'Not here, Sonya hen. We'll get them later. And we'll pick the time.'

'You . . . and what army?' I suppose I was trying to egg them on. Here in the canteen, I wanted all of them jumping on me. Boy, would they be in trouble then.

41

Wizzie knew that too. 'I'm going to make you so sorry, Driscoll.'

'In your dreams,' I said and I turned away from her. I bumped right into Zak Riley, nearly knocked his tray and his lunch all over him.

'I don't believe you!' he moaned. 'You're talking like a couple of gangsters. Did you never play with dolls?'

'No,' I said. 'Did you?'

Zak ignored that. 'Girls are supposed to be interested in pink fluffy things. Shop till you drop. Sugar and spice and all things nice?'

He had stopped in front of me. I pushed him aside. 'You're in the wrong school if you want girls like that, Zak,' I told him. 'Miss Marchmont's Academy for Young Ladies this ain't.'

I heard Wizzie laughing behind me. I couldn't help smiling either. Zak was right, I guess. Girls weren't supposed to fight, were they? But here at Cameron High, you had to be tough. You had to make sure gangs like Wizzie's knew they couldn't walk all over you.

Wizzie and her friends didn't waste any time. That same day, after school, they were gathered across the road, waiting for us. Grace stood straight when she saw us, so did Sonya. Only Wizzie ignored us, picking at her nails, calm and unconcerned. You had to admire how cool she always was. Lauren was beside her, looking as usual like an unmade bed. Had she never heard of an iron . . . or a comb?

'Wizzie's mine,' Erin whispered to me.

My heart was throbbing, I could feel the perspiration on my upper lip. But other than that no one looking at me would have known I was heading for a fight.

CHAPTER EIGHT

They spread themselves across the road, barring our way. Wizzie was right at the front, with the others close behind her. But she had her supporters too, other lowlifes from the school, ones who came from their estate, lived on the east side of the town, sympathetic to the Hell Cats. That was OK by us. We had back-up too: the ones who would step in if the fight got out of hand. I couldn't see them, but I could feel their presence, knew they would be there. They wouldn't join in the fight unless they had to. Unless the fight turned dirty.

Erin stepped a few paces ahead of me. She waved a hand at Wizzie. 'Would you mind getting out of the way? Ladies coming through.'

Wizzie just stared at her. 'Make me,' was all she said. It was all she had to say. I knew she wasn't going to move.

The wind rose and whipped up plastic cups and crisp packets and leaves across the ground. I was suddenly reminded of some old Clint Eastwood movie, the Man with No Name, staring down his enemies in a dusty Mexican street. I had to stop myself from giggling. Wizzie's eyes narrowed. I saw her as if in close-up as she stared at Erin. And Erin stared right back at her.

'She's mine,' Erin had said of her, and I knew even in that moment I was annoyed at that. Annoyed that Wizzie wasn't looking at me, searching me out. I felt guilty about it too. Erin was my very best friend.

Well, it was up to me to change things. There was going to be a fight and someone had to make the first move. It might as well be me.

I let out a roar like a demon and hurled myself towards Wizzie. Grace Morgan was as quick as I was. She threw herself between us, caught hold of my blazer and pulled me to the ground. It was then all hell broke loose. I swivelled on to my back and blocked a blow from Morgan's fist. I reached up and grabbed her by the hair. My hand almost slipped through her mane it was so greasy! But I tugged as hard as I could and she screamed.

I was aware of Lauren and Heather battling it out on

the ground beside me. And Wizzie and Erin still standing, locked in combat. And even then, in the middle of a fight, I was annoyed that it was Wizzie and Erin who were fighting each other – leader against leader – and I knew I didn't like that.

That tiny slip of concentration was all Morgan needed. She pulled herself free of me and punched me hard across the face. I saw stars, I really did, but I held on to her hair and pulled her with me as I rolled across the ground.

It was then I heard the roars and cheers from the crowd. The whole school had gathered to watch us.

At last I managed to get to my feet, but I didn't waste a moment. I didn't want to fight with Grace Morgan. I wanted Wizzie. I was sure she was getting the better of Erin.

I pushed Grace aside so hard she fell against Lauren and caught a blow meant for Heather. I yelled with laughter and turned and jumped in between Wizzie and Erin. I pulled Wizzie's head back and stopped a punch that was heading straight for my friend. Wizzie turned on me – just as I'd planned – anger flaming in her eyes. She was ready to leap at me, but she was suddenly pulled away again. Erin was on her feet, fighting

Wizzie, and I had given her the chance to get the upper hand.

Sonya was on me now. She sank her teeth into my ear. I screamed so loud that for a split second Wizzie turned to me again. A grin flashed across her face when she saw why I was screaming. I elbowed Sonya in the chest and heard her gasp for breath, but she let go of my ear. I staggered to my feet, clutching my ear. So much blood was pouring from it. The roars from the crowd were louder now, yelling at us, egging us on.

'Get right in there, Driscoll!'

'Bite off her other ear, Sonya!'

'There's nothing to beat a cat fight!'

I took a second to look around. And that's when I realised that the girls from the school had stepped to the back of the crowd, or maybe they had been pushed there. The cheering, the roaring, was all coming from the boys. We were surrounded by them. Cheering, jeering at us. I saw Zak Riley and his mates watching, taking bets on the winners.

All the boys were there.

And we were entertaining them.

'There's nothing to beat a cat fight.' The words repeated themselves in my head and made me angry.

We were the entertainment for this bunch of morons!

I pulled at Heather, hauling her off Lauren. 'Are we going to put up with this?'

Heather blinked and looked, saw what I saw: boys laughing at us, betting on us.

At the same moment, so did Lauren. She stood straight, shouted, 'Wizzie!'

Wizzie gave Erin a final push, sending her stumbling to the ground. Then she stood, legs apart, following Lauren's gaze. Erin saw it too.

Boys.

Laughing at us.

Jeering at us.

One of them shouted from the crowd, 'Don't stop now, lassies. This is great. I've got a bet on you to win, Wizzie. Get right into them!'

And a chant went up from his mates all around him.

'Win Wizzie! Win Wizzie!'

I saw Wizzie really angry then, her eyes go round as moons. She yelled back, 'This Wizzie isn't going to win for any boy!' She glanced round at her mates. Her eyes seemed to miss the rest of us. 'We don't win for anybody but us. Right?!'

'Right!' Grace Morgan yelled back.

Neither do we, I was ready to shout. But it was Erin who roared it first, and suddenly she was charging at the boys, Wizzie right by her side.

Wizzie yelled, 'Get them!'

CHAPTER NINE

Boys jumped to their feet. They leapt from the walls. They hooted with delight. But they didn't run. They stood, looking puzzled, as if they couldn't quite figure out what was going on.

I began hooting too, like some kind of wild animal, and, after a second, the others took up the chant. Some of the boys were still smiling, but the smile soon dropped from their faces as we charged towards them. Worry took its place. We began to circle them, howling like wolves, like wild female wolves.

They stepped back. 'Hey, come off it.'

'Fun's fun, but this is beyond a joke.'

'Think ye can scare us?' a weedy voice shouted.

'I think we can,' Wizzie said. She moved first. I'd never seen her move so fast. She almost leapt, and a couple of the boys stumbled and fell.

'Get them!' Erin shouted, just the second before I

planned to. Why was I always a second too late?

And we chased them. The boys turned and ran, wondering what was happening. Wondering what we would do to them if we caught them. Humiliate them, embarrass them? Maybe being chased and caught by a bunch of girls would be humiliation enough.

But the boys were determined not to be caught. I could see that in the way they ran, pulling at their friends to keep them ahead of us. They were still laughing, but there was a panic in their laughter now.

I saw little Rob Bolton squeeze through a broken rail in the school gates. His jacket caught and he pulled so hard he finally ripped his sleeve, he was that determined to get away from us. Two of the other boys threw their rucksacks over a wall and leapt after them, and got stuck on the top. I'd never seen Zak run so fast either, as if somebody had wound him up.

I was laughing as I ran. I was screaming with laughter. We were all laughing. I lifted a stone and hurled it. It smashed against a wall, narrowly missing one of the boys. He got such a fright he tripped, rolled over and ran off without even lifting his rucksack. We didn't stop chasing them until they had all disappeared. Jumping on buses, racing behind houses, vanishing into shops, belting round corners.

Finally, we stopped running. I bent over, rested my hands on my knees, trying to get my breath back.

Erin leant against a wall. 'That was brilliant.'

Rose was already fixing her hair. 'They won't laugh at us in a hurry again,' she said.

Heather was breathing so hard I thought she was hyperventilating.

I looked round for Wizzie and her crowd. They had stopped too. On the other side of the road, but miles apart from us. They gazed across. We gazed back. For a second I thought we might wave at each other, or give some kind of sign that we had beaten them. A moment of togetherness that would change everything.

But real life isn't like that.

Wizzie spat on the ground, and turned and walked away. The rest followed after her.

'That was funny though,' Heather said. 'Wizzie and them joining in, chasing them as well.'

'Had to,' Erin said at once. 'They knew they were beat. It gave them an excuse to stop fighting us.'

Heather said nothing to that.

'Have you got a problem with that?' I asked her.

She shrugged. 'It's just for once we did something together,' she said.

'They followed our lead,' I told her. 'Could never have thought of chasing the boys for themselves.'

'I suppose . . .' Then she grinned at Erin. 'I suppose you're right. They could never have thought of that for themselves.'

Erin was right? I almost yelled at her. Wasn't I the one who just said that?

Why did that always happen? Erin always got the credit.

It was all round the school next day. We had chased the boys, and the boys had run. Someone even put a photo of Erin on the school noticeboard and sketched a crown on her head. By lunchtime, she had a moustache and glasses as well. Everyone blamed Wizzie and her friends. But it was actually me. I couldn't resist it.

I met Zak Riley as he lounged outside a classroom. 'Nearly caught you yesterday, Riley. Fresh underpant time for you boys.'

'Oh aye,' Zak said. 'And what would have happened if we'd stayed and fought you? The boys are the ones who would have been blamed. Not you lot.'

I supposed in a way that was true. We were girls. We

got off with a lot more than the boys did. I didn't like it, but it happened.

Wasn't going to admit that to Zak Riley. 'Any excuse,' I said.

'You'd never have caught me anyway. I'm the best runner in the school.'

'Just as well. Who knows what we might have done if we had caught you?'

Zak stood straight, looked me right in the eye. 'What makes you like that, Hannah? Always ready for a fight. See, lassies, they're really evil.' He said it seriously. 'Boys fight wi' you. End of story. But with girls, you're never done with just a fight. You keep it up, wi' your back-stabbing and your dirty tricks. I'd hate to be a girl.'

'You'd never pass the physical,' I laughed. Zak didn't laugh back. 'Anyway, we wouldn't have you. You're not tough enough. And you're wrong about girls. We're the best. Girls are loyal. They stick by you. They don't let you down. Friends for life. Give me girls any day.'

And I meant it. So sure nothing would ever change my mind.

CHAPTER TEN

It didn't take long for word about the fight to sweep all around the school. We all got letters to take home. The ringleaders were taken into Mr McGinty's office. And guess who the ringleaders were supposed to be? Wizzie and Erin.

'I think we should all have been taken in,' I said to Heather. 'We're all just as guilty.'

Erin bounced back into the classroom as if she'd just been made head girl. 'It was old Wizzie who got most of the rollicking,' she told us later. ' "You're nothing but trouble!" McGinty told her, and when it came my turn all he said was, "Your mother will be so disappointed in you, Erin." You should have seen Wizzie's face.'

When I came home with my letter and showed it to my mum you would have thought I'd just shot JFK. She sat down at the kitchen table with the open letter in her hand. I think she watches too many soap operas –

everything she does seems like an act to me. No wonder I hardly listen to her.

'Did Erin get one of these as well?' she asked me. She answered her own question. 'I suppose her mother will be phoning me up now, saying her daughter wouldn't be in this kind of trouble if it wasn't for you. Her mother won't want you to be pals with her any more. And then where will you be?'

'Heather and Rose got letters too.'

'They're only friendly with you because Erin is. You don't want to lose Erin as a friend.'

She always made me so angry. She always made out I was lucky to have Erin as my friend, never that Erin was lucky to have me.

'You talk as if Erin was our leader . . . as if everyone listens to her and not to me.'

She looked up at me and sneered. That's the only way to describe the cruel smile that was on her face. 'You're like me, Hannah. Nobody listens to you either. I'm a loser, and if you go on like this,' – she waved the letter about as if it was on fire – 'you'll end up a loser too.'

There was no way I was going to sit and listen to anyone, even my mother, calling me a loser. I stood up and stormed off to my room. 'Come back here, Hannah. I'm still talking to you.'

But I didn't go back and she didn't follow me. I marched into my room and slammed the door shut. I was on the phone to Erin right away. Her number was engaged. A moment later my phone rang. Heather's number. 'I thought it was you who was on the phone to Erin. It must be Rose.'

So we'd all phoned Erin first. I was every bit as bad as the rest. But Erin was *my* best friend, wasn't she?

'Did your mother go spare?' Heather asked.

In the 'going spare' stakes, my mother always won hands down.

'Mine too,' Heather said. 'But she blamed it all on Wizzie. I told them we had no choice but to fight back, and they believed me. It was self-defence, I told her. My mum said violence doesn't solve anything, and my dad said it was good I could stick up for myself. Now they're not talking to each other. It's hilarious.'

Heather wanted us all to come over to her place. But by the time I got hold of Erin – how long had she been on the phone to Rose and what could they possibly have to say to each other? – it was too late. Rose's parents were angry. They'd got together to discuss it, but blamed her brother, who was in the school too, for not looking after her properly. And as for Erin, her mother had sat her down and discussed the whole thing with her, and told her not to let it happen again. In fact, her mum did all the things they would tell a mum to do in one of those agony columns. I'm telling you, Erin's mum is perfect. All she seemed worried about was how this would affect Erin and her grades.

'Want to swap mothers?' I said, only half joking.

'Take your mother? I don't want to be cruel, Hannah . . . but I'd rather have my teeth drilled without anaesthetic.' Erin said it for a laugh. But I couldn't laugh. I knew it was too near the truth.

'Mum wants to just forget about it, and I don't blame her.' Erin was changing the subject. 'She's got enough on her plate with Avril's wedding.'

Avril's wedding . . . I was looking forward to it too. My first chance to get all dressed up and go on a big night out with my friends.

Didn't know it was going to change my life.

CHAPTER ELEVEN

The morning of the wedding Junior Bonnar was at his door, throwing confetti over me and Mum. Junior has been our next-door neighbour for as far back as I can remember. He used to live with his mum, but she died a few years ago and I was surprised that Junior was allowed to stay in the house. I won't say there's anything wrong with Junior, but he is definitely one sandwich short of a picnic. I mean, he holds down a job – and he drives a car, very badly, I might add. He's even taught me how to drive . . . just as badly. But in spite of all of that, you know that there is something not quite right about him.

Mum actually does a lot for him. Washes his clothes and irons them, and makes sure he's eating the right kind of food.

'Oh, Terry,' he said when he saw me emerge from our flat. 'You look lovely. You're that grown-up looking.'

That's what I mean about there being something not quite right about Junior. He calls me Terry. He's lived next door for years, but for some reason he still can't get my name right. Terry, he always calls me.

I don't even correct him any more. 'Thanks, Junior.'

'And you too, Mrs Driscoll. You're a doll.'

'I'm not going to the wedding, Junior,' Mum told him. 'These are my working clothes.'

Didn't bother Junior. He only grinned. 'You're still a doll.'

'I think he fancies you, Mum,' I said, as we went downstairs.

'That makes him a definite case for care in the community then.'

That was so typical of Mum. She could never accept a compliment with any grace. She always turned it into an insult.

It was one of those real West of Scotland days, with battleship-grey clouds hanging so low you felt you could reach up and sink your hands into them. They hovered above us, threatening at any minute to open up and flood us with a downpour. 'Don't you dare ruin my hair!' I yelled at them, as we stood outside the church, waiting for the bride to arrive.

'Or my dress!' Heather added. She was resplendent in pink. A bit too much like a marshmallow, if you asked me.

Rose looked gorgeous in petrol blue. She always looked older than the rest of us. She even had boobs, big ones too.

I was wearing a green jacket and skirt. My mum had already told me green just wasn't my colour. Now she was hanging about outside the church doors with her camera, gushing compliments on the wedding party as each of them arrived in their taxis – much to my embarrassment.

'What a lovely mother of the bride you make,' she gushed at Erin's mother.

Personally I thought Erin's mum looked ridiculous. Her hat was like a spaceship. 'Did she land in that thing?' I whispered to Heather. Every time she turned her head she almost knocked someone out.

My mother just couldn't give up. 'Though you hardly look old enough to be the mother of the bride.'

If my mother thought she was getting round Mrs Brodie with compliments she was wrong. But that didn't stop my mum. 'Such a lovely outfit. And look at our Erin! Isn't she just lovely?'

Erin's mum turned away with a tight smile. 'Our Erin' whispered to me, 'You poor thing, Hannah. You must be so embarrassed.'

I knew what she meant. I felt like yelling at her. 'Shut up, Mum!' I wanted her away from here altogether.

When Avril arrived Mum was even worse. She shouted over everyone's head, 'She's like a fairy-tale princess.'

Personally, I thought Avril looked more like a meringue. But I didn't say. I ooh-ed and ah-ed with the rest of them, and was so glad my mum had to go off to work before the church ceremony. I only relaxed once she'd gone.

The rain held off until we were all on the bus taking the guests to the hotel on the river, where the reception was being held. Then it came down like a torrent. But the weather didn't matter by that time. The photographs had been taken and everyone was in a mood to party.

There was champagne laid out in the hotel foyer on our arrival – unfortunately we were only allowed orange juice. We clocked right away to see if there would be any boys there, but Erin had already warned us that, apart from her brother's friends, she only had two spotty male cousins, and if the groom was anything to go by, his family had only just learnt how to walk upright.

'Straight out of the trees,' I said.

'Trust you, Hannah!' Heather giggled. 'I'm ready for a laugh.'

'We're going to have a laugh . . . One a minute, OK?'

At that point Rose got herself locked in one of the toilets and had to be rescued, and we knew the night had begun.

We were given a table to ourselves at the meal.

'Look who's serving at the top table!' I said. It was Lauren's older sister. There was a distinct family resemblance. Lauren's sister just looked cleaner. 'She's being so rude!' You couldn't help but notice the way she stared at people as they spoke to her. 'If she looks at me like that I'll punch her.'

'Please,' Heather said with a giggle. 'No violence.'

Lauren's sister, and everything else that might spoil our night, was soon forgotten. The meal was wonderful, and in between the starter and the main course, a haggis was piped in. We tasted each other's food and declared everything more delicious than anything we had ever tasted before. We couldn't stop giggling like idiots. Erin was stuck at the top table and kept waving at us and mouthing, 'Wish I was there.'

I couldn't blame her. The best man, sitting next to her, looked like he'd just been let out for the day from the local zoo. After the meal the speeches began and we sneaked off, deciding it would be more fun to be stuck in the toilets again. By the time we came out the tables had been cleared and pushed to the sides of the room and the band were setting up to play.

Erin's mum came up to us and led us to a table. 'You sit here, girls,' she said. 'I'm so glad you could all be here today. I wanted all Erin's friends to be with her.'

Now that she'd taken off her massive hat she was left with a ring round her hair. She didn't seem to care. She was on a high. 'Now, you girls enjoy yourselves. Just ask when you want more orange juice.'

I shook my head. 'If I drink any more orange juice I'll turn orange myself. And that just doesn't go with green.'

She giggled. 'I'm going to send over a bowl of non-alcoholic punch to your table. How does that sound? But if you fancy anything else you can get it at the bar.'

'Whisky, gin, vodka?' I suggested.

It took her a moment to see I was only joking, then she laughed again. 'What a girl you are, Hannah!'

'She is so nice,' Heather said as we watched her stagger off in her high heels to the next table.

'My mum and her have started going to yoga together,' Rose said.

'I know. That's the yoga class my mum goes to,' Heather added.

'I'll have to get Mrs Driscoll to join them.' I didn't want to be left out. But we all knew that would never happen. Everyone avoided my mum like the plague. I could watch people cross to the other side of the street to avoid her. I understood that. If she hadn't been my mother, I'd have done it too.

Erin swished towards us in her bridesmaid's dress. 'Having a nice time?' She squeezed herself into a chair beside me. 'Did you see who was serving at my table?'

We told her we had.

'I kept looking out to make sure she wasn't spitting in my soup,' she said.

'She was being so rude.'

Erin agreed with me at once. 'You're telling me! I shouted after her to get more crusty bread and she totally ignored me. How she was allowed to serve at the top table I'll never know.' She pulled up her dress and took off her shoes and began rubbing her toes. 'My feet are killing me and I've got to dance with the best man.'

We looked across the hall and there he was, waving at her. He was the drippiest-looking guy I had ever seen, and to make things worse he was wearing a kilt.

'If I had legs like that I'd have them amputated.' I giggled. 'They look like a couple of matchsticks under a pelmet.'

I think he heard because he turned and glared at me. Either that or he was really constipated.

Erin's brother, Calum, brought our special bowl of punch to us. 'Just for you, girls,' he said. Calum was dishy, but not interested in any of us, of course. He was with his mates and they all moved off in search of good-looking female guests.

After the first waltz, Erin was finally free to join us. She ladled punch into her glass and we all giggled and laughed and talked about everyone at the wedding.

Just for a moment, I sat back in my chair. Everyone in the hall seemed to become just shadows in the background. The lights dimmed and the music faded. My friends were leaning across the table, laughing. It was as if we were the only real people in the room.

And I thought to myself, *This is the best night of my life*.

CHAPTER TWELVE

The night just seemed to get better after that.

The band announced there had been a request for Rose to go up to sing. It was actually me who requested it, though I didn't tell her that. She was over the moon. She tried to pretend she was mortified, couldn't possibly sing in front of all these people, but she was up on that stage before you could say *Pop Idol*.

She sang 'Summer Lovin'. I knew she would. She'd been practising it for ages. It was the song she planned to sing at the audition for the school show, although as Rose liked to inform us, the actual title was 'Summer Nights'. 'Summer Nights' or 'Summer Lovin', she managed to squeeze in two more verses – I think she made them up. The band began to think she was never getting off the stage, so they finally stopped playing and she had to shut up. We leapt to our feet when she'd finished, cheering and clapping and stamping our feet enthusiastically.

'If she sings like that at the auditions, she'll definitely get the part of Sandy,' Erin said. 'She's not got any competition anyway. She's the best singer in the school.'

We were up for every dance after that, from the Slosh to the Highland Fling. As soon as the music started we were up there, in the middle of the floor, causing havoc, knocking people over, laughing ourselves silly.

At the line dancing they started getting really annoyed at us. Erin and I were pushed off the floor.

'Some people are trying to dance here,' one of the guests said. The man had changed into cowboy boots and a ten-gallon hat. Considering he was also still wearing his kilt, he looked ridiculous.

'How can you take this seriously?' I yelled back at him.

When we got back to our table, Calum had brought us more punch. 'This is great stuff,' I told him. 'I don't normally like lemonade.'

Calum and his pals laughed so much I thought they were about to have a fit. 'Maybe the vodka's got something to do with it.'

They all walked away, still laughing. I looked at Erin. For the first time I noticed her eyes were crossed. 'Did he say vodka?'

'My mum'll kill him if she finds that out,' she said, taking another sip.

We watched Heather and Rose stumbling about on the dance floor, tumbling against people, annoying everyone.

'I don't think he's kidding. I think it is vodka he put in there. No wonder we're having so much fun.' That only made us giggle all the more. 'Don't tell them,' I said, pointing at Heather and Rose.

Then we both giggled. The country music stopped at last. The daft line dancers reluctantly left the floor, and we were suddenly grabbed by two of Erin's uncles and pulled on to the floor for a Gay Gordons. If you don't know what that is, it's a dance that includes a lot of twirling and birling, and halfway through I saw Erin's face turn as green as my outfit.

'Are you OK?'

She shook her head. 'I think I'm going to be sick.'

Her uncle positively threw her at me, as if she was ready to vomit all over his kilt. I grabbed her and led her to the toilets. 'It must be that vodka,' I said.

'I don't feel well, Hannah.'

Erin just made it into a cubicle before she emptied

her whole stomach. She knelt on the floor with her head in the bowl, and I sat beside her and rubbed her back as she threw up. What are friends for? Finally, she slumped against the wall, exhausted. Her skin was the colour of wax and her face was covered in sweat. I wet some paper towels and dabbed at her face to cool her down. Then I slid to the floor beside her.

'Feel better?' I asked.

She nodded.

'It's been a great night, hasn't it?'

'Up till now,' Erin said softly.

'Not your fault you were sick,' I said.

'You're a great friend, Hannah.'

I only shrugged my shoulders. 'And you're a great friend. The best.'

'Do you mean that?' she said, suddenly more serious. 'You're supposed to have only one best friend, did you know that? There's four of us. So which one of us would you say was your best friend?'

Was she testing me? What did she want me to say? I knew what I wanted to say. Erin. I wanted Erin to be my best friend. I thought of her as my best friend, but I had a feeling we all did. So I wouldn't say it. I'd die of embarrassment if she said she preferred Heather or Rose.

But she didn't.

'You're mine,' she confessed. 'I've always thought you and me are special.'

That was how I felt too, how I'd always felt. 'I think so too,' I said. 'But what about Heather and Rose?'

'They're great . . . almost best friends. But I couldn't be best friends with Rose. She's so vain. Her best friend's her mirror. And as for Heather . . . let's face it. She's lovely, but a bit thick, don't you think so? She's just not in our league, Hannah. She's not as smart as you and me. I mean, she never gets a joke. Haven't you noticed that?'

How true was that? I agreed with Erin eagerly.

'But you're the best, Hannah.' She hugged me so tightly, I could hardly breathe.

'You'd probably say the same thing to Rose or Heather if they were here instead of me.'

She pushed me away from her. 'No, I would not,' she said. 'Don't you believe me?'

'I want to.'

'Do you want me to prove it?' she said suddenly.

'What do you mean, "prove it"?' And I giggled.

'What if I tell you something I've never told anybody else in my whole life? A secret.' Her voice quivered.

71

'The seventh magpie. Do you know what the seventh magpie is, Hannah?'

'One for sorrow, two for joy, three for a girl, and four for a boy –'

Erin took it up. 'Five for silver, six for gold –'

I finished it for her. 'Seven for a secret never to be told . . .'

'That's right.' What she actually said was. 'Thatsright.' She was slurring her words. Her eyes were hooded. She looked as if she was about to fall asleep. I realised she must be drunk. Talking rubbish, I thought.

'A secret?' I said. 'What secret can you possibly have?'

She began to bite at her knuckles nervously. 'Have you never wondered how I don't ever sleep over . . . anywhere?'

'You hate leaving your mum.' It was the reason she always gave. I had never doubted it. 'And your mum can't bear the thought of not having her wee Erin in the house.'

Erin shook her head. Her face was so grey now I thought she was going to be sick again. 'There's another reason.'

Now I was intrigued. 'What reason?'

She began waving her hands about. 'No . . . no! Big

mistake if I tell. Let the circle be unbroken. That's what my mum always says.' She was trying to stop herself from telling me all. But by now, she really had me hooked. A secret. A secret never to be told.

'Oh, come on, Erin. You can't stop now. What is it? Wait a minute . . .' I giggled. 'You're really a family of aliens, studying humans, and you all turn into fat ugly gits at midnight.'

'I wish,' she said, and she began giggling too. 'I wish it was something as simple as that. If I tell, you've got to promise never to tell. On your mother's life. On your life. Never to tell anybody. It's still a secret. Right? Our secret.'

I crossed my heart. I even crossed my eyes and that made Erin laugh again. But her eyes were nipped with tears.

'What is it?' I asked, desperate now to know.

Still she held back, bit her lip. It was almost as if she was in pain. She was finding it hard to say the words. But I knew she wouldn't not tell me now.

'Oh, it's so embarrassing.' And Erin blushed and I'd never seen Erin blush before.

'You won't embarrass me,' I said, and I clutched at her hand.

'The reason I don't sleep over anywhere is because . . .' There she went again with the long pause. 'Because I wet the bed.'

CHAPTER THIRTEEN

I was totally gobsmacked. 'You do . . . what?'

Now she'd said it, she couldn't stop everything else from tumbling out. 'I still wet the bed. Almost every night. I hate myself. I don't know why. My mum even had me at a child psychologist . . . Nothing worked. I still wet the bed. It's so embarrassing.'

For a moment I didn't know what to say. It was the last thing I'd expected. Then before I could stop myself, I started laughing.

Erin was horrified. She tried to spring to her feet till she remembered she was drunk. She was almost crying. 'Hannah!'

I couldn't stop laughing. I lay along the floor of the toilets. 'I thought you were going to tell me something earth-shattering . . . You've got two weeks to live . . . Your mother's had a sex change operation and she's really your dad . . . Anything . . . And what do you tell me? . . . You wet the bed . . . I'm nearly wetting myself now . . . *pssssh* . . .' I made a sound like running water.

Erin didn't know what to do. She was watching me, hate and puzzlement in her eyes. I pulled her close and hugged her.

'Erin . . . It's not the end of the world. And I promise I'll never tell. Cross my heart and hope to die.'

Erin smiled, unsurely, then she began laughing too. 'But you've really got to mean it. You'll never tell. I'd die if anybody else found out.'

At that moment I wished so much I had a secret I could share with Erin. But even my mother's secret was something everyone knew of, but never talked about. My life was an open book. I couldn't come up with a thing. 'I'll never tell,' I said. 'Never in a hundred million years. I swear on my mother's grave.'

'Your mother's not dead,' Erin reminded me.

'I'll go home and murder her tonight and bury her. OK?'

That made her laugh again. 'You promise? Oh, please, please, don't tell.'

'Never,' I said, as I helped her to her feet. '*Pssshhhh* . . .' I said again. '*Psshhh*.'

She stopped me. 'You've got to promise this is the

last time we'll ever talk about this. You'll never mention it again. It'll be as if I never told you in the first place.'

I knew then I could never joke about it with her. Not ever again. It was too embarrassing for her. I pulled a zip across my lips. 'Never again.'

We were arm in arm as we came out of the toilets. I'd never felt so close to Erin as I did that night. Erin had trusted me with her secret. A secret never to be told. No one else. No doubt about it now. I was Erin's best friend.

Heather was waiting for us at the door of the toilets, ready to drag us back into the middle of the dance floor. 'They're going to play "Loch Lomond"!' she screamed. 'I thought you were going to miss it.'

We all gathered round in a circle ready to sing and dance. I grasped Erin's hand as the music began and squeezed. Our secret, a secret never to be told. My best friend had trusted her secret to me. And I would never break that trust.

CHAPTER FOURTEEN

My mum wanted to know everything about the wedding next morning at breakfast. I had a splitting headache and a mouth like the bottom of a budgie's cage. I kept thinking about the vodka Calum said he'd put in the punch and wondered if I might have a hangover. If this was a hangover I promised myself I would never drink again.

'Did you have a wonderful time?'

I nodded, and felt as if a brass bell was clanging inside my head. 'Great,' I muttered.

'Erin looked lovely,' Mum said dreamily. 'She fair suits that colour with her lovely golden hair. She's a real strawberry blonde.' She looked at me then, at my hair, and I knew she was comparing us and I was coming off worse. My hand automatically moved to my head. Mousey, my mum always called my hair. I told myself I didn't care. I could dye it when I was older.

'Never mind,' Mum said. She was obviously reading my mind. 'You can dye yours the same colour when you're older.' Then she carried on as if that shouldn't hurt me. 'I'm glad you enjoyed yourself. Your first grown-up night out without your mother tagging along. That's a night to remember.'

And of course, it was a night to remember, but for a different reason.

Erin's secret. No wonder she was ashamed to tell anyone. Erin was always so sure of herself, so cool. If anyone found out about that, she'd never be cool again. Everything about Erin fell into place now. No school trips, no sleepovers, never a night away from her mother.

And I was the only one she had entrusted with her secret. It made me feel special.

I phoned her later that afternoon, didn't mention what she'd told me. We'd never talk of it again, I had told her, and I meant it. But it had brought a closeness between us that we didn't have to put into words.

'Want to come over to my place later?' she asked me.

'Sure. Want me to phone the others?'

'No,' she said. 'Just for a change, it'll be you and me.'

And now I knew I was really special.

It seemed to me that I was on top of the world when I went to school next day. The whole gang of us met at the front gates as usual, but it was my arm Erin linked in hers. And if Heather and Rose noticed, they didn't say.

Wizzie and her gang were waiting for us in the corridor, blocking our way. 'Heard the bride was a dog,' Wizzie said.

Lauren had to get her bit in too. 'She was nothing to the groom. It was not so much losing a daughter, as gaining a monkey.'

I remembered then that Lauren's sister had been one of the waitresses. She probably told them everything about the wedding. 'Jealousy's a terrible thing,' I said, and to Erin I added, 'Wizzie hasn't a hope in hell getting married. Who'd have her?'

Heather came charging up to me after registration. 'Were you at Erin's last night?'

Rose was right behind her. 'Without us? How come you didn't phone us?'

'It was a last-minute thing,' I said. 'We don't have to do everything together.'

But I knew I would have been miffed too if I'd been the one left out.

'Sorry,' I said. 'I should have thought.' I took the blame and was immediately angry at myself. It was just what my mum would have done, always the first one to apologise. So I added. 'But for goodness' sake, we're not joined at the hip.'

It took the rest of the day for them to come round. In a way, I understood, but still I told myself, it wasn't as if I'd committed murder.

But by the time we linked up after school we were all friends again, laughing and joking as we walked home.

I didn't know then that it would be the last time we would ever be together . . . as friends.

CHAPTER FIFTEEN

It began like an ordinary day. I got up, had breakfast, went to school in the rain. I had an argument with Zak Riley. Not a hint anything was about to happen. I can't be very psychic, can I? Or I would surely have felt it, seen it coming.

I was in the changing room in the gym, just finished netball practice. It was the only thing I did without the others. I was sweating buckets, laughing with the rest of the team, when suddenly, the door swung open and Erin stood there. She was blazing with anger, her eyes locked on mine. I leapt to my feet.

'What's happened, Erin?'

A silence fell in the changing room. What you might call 'an ominous silence'. I know that now. It seemed an age before anything happened.

I asked again, 'What is it, Erin?'

I saw then that her eyes had tears in them. As if she

was desperately wanting to cry and determined not to. I took a step forward, sure it had to be a problem with Wizzie and her gang.

Erin didn't answer me. As I moved, so did she, leaping towards me, bringing her hand up hard and slapping me right across the face. She took me so much by surprise I stumbled, lost my footing and fell back across a bench. My face stung.

'Erin!' It was all I could say. 'Erin!'

'You bitch!'

And then Rose was behind her, pulling her back. She was glaring at me too. 'She's not worth it, Erin,' she said.

'Is this a joke?' I got back on my feet unsteadily, totally confused about what was going on.

'Maybe it is to you.' And with that Erin broke free of Rose and rushed at me again. She gave me such a punch that once again I went down in a tumble of arms and legs. Now it wasn't just Rose who was holding Erin back. The rest of the netball team were grabbing at her too. Erin couldn't hold back the tears then. They popped from her eyes like bubbles and tumbled down her cheeks. 'I hate you, Hannah Driscoll. I've never hated anyone as much as I hate you.'

Then Rose dragged her out of the changing rooms and slammed the door shut behind her.

'What was that all about?' someone asked.

'Oooo, annoyed your leader, have you?'

'She's not my leader!' I snapped the words out. I was almost crying myself. She's my friend, I wanted to say, but after what had just happened I wasn't so sure any more. I scrambled to my feet, didn't even bother changing out of my shorts. I ran out after Erin. I couldn't see her, but I could hear the noise coming from round the corner. Lots of noise, laughing and jeering, and Wizzie's voice was above it all.

'Keep back, it might be catching!' I heard her say.

As I turned the corner, Erin was surrounded by Wizzie and her gang. Rose was hugging her, shielding her, trying to steer her through the giggling crowd of girls. I ran towards them, ready to do battle, protect Erin too – stopped dead when I heard what they were all shouting.

'*Pssh* . . .' Wizzie giggled and the rest took up the chant. '*Pssshhhh*, Erin.'

'Better go and empty your incontinence knickers!' Grace Morgan shouted.

'*Pssshhhh!*'

They knew. They all knew. But how?

I ran after Erin, shouting her name over and over. 'It wasn't me, Erin. Honest. It wasn't me!'

And suddenly, Erin turned on me and spat right in my face. 'Who else could it be? I've never told anybody else in my entire life.'

Heather came hurrying up the corridor, pushing everyone aside to get to Erin. She must have heard the commotion, but she didn't seem to understand what was going on. All she could see was a friend in need. She put her arms round Erin, and I watched her face drain to grey when she heard what the others were chanting.

'Who else could it be?' Erin said again. 'I should never have trusted you.'

Heather's eyes darted to me – me, separate from my friends, left out in the cold – and her arms went tighter round Erin.

My friends were suddenly gone. They moved away, and I was alone in the corridor with my enemies.

I swirled round to Wizzie. 'It's a lie! What you're saying about her, it's a lie!'

Her eyebrow, and the pierced ring that was in it, shot up. 'Who are you trying to kid? It's all round the school. You only have to say one wee word . . . *Pssssshhhh.*' She made the sound again, the sound I had made myself in

85

the toilets at the wedding. 'And your pal knows exactly what everybody means. As soon as she heard it she wet herself.' Then she began to laugh like a hyena. She turned to her friends. 'Get it, girls. She wet herself.' Then she looked back at me and her face became serious. 'No lie, Hannah, old chum. Miss Perfect ain't so perfect.'

'Who told you?' I wanted to know, had to know. I had to tell Erin, then we could get whoever it was, take them on together.

But all Wizzie said was, 'Good news travels fast.' And she was gone, swaggering off with her giggling friends. They were all enjoying the joke.

How could they be so cruel? It wasn't anything to laugh about. Who could have told them? And Erin's words came back to me like a slap in the face.

Who else but me?

Erin had told me her secret. A secret she had never shared with anyone else. We'd been alone, sitting on the floor of the hotel toilets. No one else had been in there.

But someone must have been there. Someone must have overheard.

And I was going to find out who!

CHAPTER SIXTEEN

Erin wasn't in the next class. Neither was Rose. There was an outright laugh when the teacher told us that Erin wasn't feeling well and had to be sent home. Heather sat in front of me, back straight, ignoring me no matter how I tried to get her attention. I even sent a couple of rubbers flying in her direction – but nothing would make her turn round to me. She couldn't ignore me in the corridor. I stood in front of her and wouldn't let her pass.

'Heather, you've got to convince Erin that I never told a soul. Not a soul.'

Heather kept glancing around her. She looked scared, as if she was afraid someone would catch her talking to me and pass the word back to Erin. 'Erin says you're the only person in the world she told. Only you.' She paused. 'Who else could it be?'

She tried to move round me but I blocked her way.

'I would never have told anybody. It was a secret. You have to make her see that.'

Heather pushed past me. She couldn't even look me in the eye. 'I'll try,' she said.

'Please, Heather. Please. You've got to convince her.'

She looked back at me for a second. I felt she wanted to stay, to say something else, talk to me, be my friend. Then she bit her lip to stop any words from spilling out. Only as she hurried away I heard her mumble again, 'I'll try.'

It was the most miserable day of my life. I went over the night of the wedding again and again in my head. Erin being sick, both of us running to the ladies, sitting on the floor, telling secrets. Could anyone else have been there? Hiding in one of the cubicles?

I closed my eyes, remembering every detail. The doors were all open, no feet hidden underneath, and there was an empty feel to the place. I could still hear in my head the sounds of the music playing in the hall, people laughing and singing, and in the toilets, our voices echoing in the emptiness, just me and Erin and her secret.

Someone else had to have been there. But who?

I tried constantly, every spare moment I had, to

phone Erin on my mobile. Each time there was no answer. I knew she would see my number displayed and not pick up.

As soon as I got home I used the land line, withholding my number this time. It was her mother who answered the phone.

'Mrs Brodie, can I speak to Erin, please?' Even I could hear the desperation in my voice.

I couldn't miss the ice in Mrs Brodie's. 'You have some nerve phoning here. Call yourself a friend? Erin hasn't stopped crying since she came home. Was that your idea of fun? Telling everybody such a thing? I know you've got a warped sense of humour, but surely even you know when to draw the line.'

I was so taken aback by the venom in her voice I couldn't even interrupt to defend myself. And then, in the background, I heard another voice. Erin's voice.

'Is that her, Mum? Hang up on her. I never want to talk to her again.'

'Erin!!!!' I screamed it through the phone. 'It wasn't me.' But by that time, the line was dead.

I was crying when my mum came home from work. 'What on earth's wrong with you?'

I wished I could have told her the whole truth, let it

all pour out to someone. But Mum was the last person I would confide in. 'I had a falling out with Erin,' was all I said.

She accepted it without a quibble. 'Och well, give her a phone, apologise, make up. You'll be friends again by tomorrow.'

And in a way, that made me feel better. Tomorrow I would make Erin listen. I'd make her see that I could never have broken her trust. I went to bed that night, but I didn't sleep. I tossed and I turned and I prayed. I prayed that tomorrow I was going to be able to make everything all right.

I stood at the school gates waiting for her to arrive, but she didn't come. Maybe, I thought, she wasn't coming again today. Then another thought jumped on that. Maybe she was never coming back. She'd been transferred to another school, one that knew nothing of her 'secret'.

But she did come. I was sitting in class when she arrived. She strode into the classroom, with Rose on one side of her and Heather on the other, for protection. I should have been there too, I thought. I tried to catch her eye, but she totally blanked me.

As soon as Erin sat down, Wizzie whispered, '*Psssh-hhh*,' and the whole class giggled.

Mrs Tasker, the teacher, yelled out, 'If I hear any-thing like that again there will be trouble.'

And I realised then that the teachers knew the whole story. Erin was being 'looked after' by them as well. I knew too, by the way Mrs Tasker turned her eyes to glare at me, exactly who she blamed for it all. Me.

I looked away. I knew it made me look guilty but I couldn't help it. Everyone was blaming me, and I hadn't done anything.

At break, Mrs Tasker made us all stay in our seats until she'd escorted Erin and Rose and Heather out of the class. Wizzie couldn't keep her mouth shut even then.

'Ooo, have your friends fallen out with you, Driscoll? Cause you've got a big mouth?'

I squared up to her. 'It wasn't me and you know it.'

'If it wasn't you . . . who else could it be?'

It was Lauren who said that, poking her face in between us. Then she bellowed with laughter and grabbed at Wizzie's arm and off they went.

I stood there watching them and I realised I knew the answer.

Lauren's sister had been a waitress at the wedding.

She had glared at us all the time she was serving. She'd ignored Erin at the top table.

Lauren's sister must have been listening outside the toilet doors while Erin was baring her soul to me.

Lauren's sister was the one to blame.

CHAPTER SEVENTEEN

All I could think about was telling Erin, but I couldn't find any of them anywhere. It seemed the teachers had her well protected. It wasn't until lunchtime that I saw them coming into the canteen. Erin had purple shadows under her eyes, as if she hadn't stopped crying. Rose strode beside her like some fierce warrior guard, daring anyone to say a word to her. Heather padded behind them. She looked worried, as if she'd been crying too. The weakest link, that was Heather. Rose and Erin took their seats at our table. I knew I couldn't get near Erin, but as soon as I saw Heather going up to the counter to wait in the queue I was there beside her. I felt as if every eye in the canteen was on us. I didn't care.

'I've got to talk to Erin, Heather.' Her eyes darted across to the table where Erin sat with Rose. They were both watching us closely. I could almost feel Erin's icy stare go through me like a dagger. I clutched at

Heather's arm. 'I've found out who spread that story, and she has to know it wasn't me.'

Heather's face went pale. She pulled away from me, but I had to make her believe me. 'You must know it wasn't me, Heather.'

She shrugged, didn't even look at me, and I was sure then that deep down Heather did believe me.

'It was Lauren's sister,' I said.

Heather's eyes flashed at me. 'Who?'

'You remember she was there? She was serving at the top table, remember? She was a waitress. She must have overheard Erin. It was her!'

Heather stared at me as if she was taking it all in. Then, with a sigh, she actually smiled at me. 'Of course. Of course. It must have been her.'

I smiled back. Friends again.

Just then Rose came up and tugged at Heather's arm. 'Don't talk to her.'

Heather grabbed at her. 'No, wait, Rose. You've got to listen. Hannah knows who spread it . . . and it wasn't her.'

Rose wasn't the one I wanted to convince and for once Erin was alone and unprotected. I pushed them both aside and ran to her table and threw myself on the seat beside her. 'It was Lauren's sister!' I said at once, terrified someone would stop me before I could get it out. 'She must have heard you. Listened at the toilet door or something. She's told Lauren and that's how it got all round the school.'

I could tell Erin was trying to take all this in. She must have realised this was a much more logical solution than her best friend letting her down. Finally, she snapped at me. 'You better not be making this up, Driscoll.'

I saw them coming into the canteen just then, Wizzie and the rest of the Hell Cats, pushing their way through the doors, taking up too much room.

I stood up, pulling at Erin's sleeve. 'There she is. There's Lauren. Let's ask her. She'll have guilt written all over her face. She won't be able to deny it.'

And I was sure no one would believe her even if she did.

Once again, I felt like one of them, a Lip Gloss Girl, ready to confront Wizzie with my friends at my back, afraid of nothing. It was all going to be all right. I balled my fist ready to punch Lauren. That's how angry I was.

They stopped in their tracks as they saw us storming towards them. I only halted when I was inches away from Lauren's face. I spat the words out at her. 'It was your sister, wasn't it?'

Lauren looked at Wizzie as if I'd spoken in a foreign language.

'At least have the courage to admit it was her. She was listening at the door of the ladies, wasn't she? Heard Erin telling me. She's the one who spread it, isn't she? She told you, and you told everybody else.' I hated the desperation and the anger in my voice. I couldn't stop it.

Lauren took a step back and peered at me, her eyes half shut. 'You think my sister told me that your pal, Erin here, pishes the bed . . . and I spread it about. Is that it?'

I had wanted her to look guilty. But she didn't. Her kind wouldn't. She probably thought there was nothing wrong in what she'd done. Lauren just looked amused. As if it was a great joke.

'My sister?' she said. 'She heard you talking in the toilets? She was outside the ladies and you were inside and she was listening? Is that your story?'

Erin was right behind me. I could feel her tense herself. Ready for a fight.

I wanted to show her I was her friend, her best

friend. 'Yes, your scabby sister. She was a waitress, and not a very good one.' I tried to use some of my old boldness. *By tonight*, I thought, *we'll all be at Erin's house, laughing about this*. Everything would have been explained and I would have punched Lauren's front teeth halfway down her throat. 'She was standing at the door of the ladies' listening to everything we said.' I could picture it so clearly in my mind's eye, it had to be the truth. 'And then she couldn't wait to tell you, because she knows you've got such a big mouth.'

Wizzie was sneering in what would have passed for her as a smile. There was a weight like a bowling ball in the pit of my stomach. Why couldn't they just admit that was what had happened?

Wizzie turned to Lauren. 'Will you tell her, or will I?' she said.

'Oh, let me, Wizzie.' And Lauren looked at me and she smiled triumphantly. That's the only way I could describe that smile. Triumphant. Then she went on. 'My sister couldn't have heard you if you'd used a megaphone. My sister's deaf.'

CHAPTER EIGHTEEN

Deaf.

From somewhere in the back of my mind flashed a picture of Lauren's sister at the wedding. The way she stared at people, I had thought she was being so rude. Now I realised she had been reading people's lips, studying their faces. And she hadn't ignored Erin. She simply hadn't heard her.

Deaf.

It hadn't been her sister after all. Couldn't have been. But who else?

I didn't get time to think it out. I was suddenly punched in the head. It was Erin. 'You lying cow! You nearly had me falling for that. I hate you.'

I tried to talk to her, but she spat in my face. 'You're worse than them,' she nodded at Wizzie. 'At least they've got an excuse for being retards.'

I expected Wizzie to leap at her for saying that. But

she didn't. Instead, she settled herself on top of the table and crossed her legs. 'This is so much fun. The Lip Gloss Girls are fighting amongst themselves.' Then she laughed. 'Better hurry, Erin. Those incontinence knickers only hold so much.'

She clapped her hands as Erin turned away from her, but this time Erin wasn't crying. She was too angry to cry. 'I'll get you for that, Wizzie.' Then her eyes moved to me and there was hate in them. 'And I'll get you as well. You wait and see if I don't.'

I walked through the rest of the day in a dream. No, a nightmare. I couldn't concentrate on anything. All I wanted to do was cry. How was I going to convince Erin that I would never have betrayed her? She wouldn't even look at me, and I couldn't get near her. She was always surrounded, not just by Rose and Heather, but by other girls on the edges of our gang. Geraldine Mooney, always wanting to be one of us, suddenly was. She stood in front of Erin, glaring at me.

I tried texting Erin, but she wouldn't answer, and I knew when she saw my number coming up on her phone she would just ignore it.

I tried to text her again, at break, and for a moment, just a moment, I thought she was going to answer me.

We were in the English corridor, and she stared at my text and then she stared at me, and started walking towards me, holding the phone in her hand. She came so close to me, I thought she must have forgiven me, believed me at last. She stopped inches from my face and held the phone in front of me so I could see my message clearly on the screen. Then, with the press of a button, the text was gone.

'Erased!' Erin snapped at me. 'Your message, and you. Erased from my life, for ever.'

She had erased me from her life. And not just Erin. All of them had erased me. That's what made it so hard. I had no one to talk to, no one to confide in. And I so wanted someone to talk to. These were my friends, my best friends. Friends for ever. And now, suddenly, I had none of them in my life.

At home that night I didn't eat any dinner and went straight to my room. Mum came in to see me before she went to bed. She couldn't fail to see I'd been crying. The soaking pillow and puffy eyes were a dead give-away. 'Are you OK? Still not made up with Erin?'

I wished I could tell her, but if I did there was no knowing how she would react.

'I was watching a sad film on TV,' I said.

And she believed me. 'You shouldn't get yourself into a state about a film on TV.' She shook her head. 'Real life's bad enough.'

I had never agreed with my mum about that till that moment. I'd always thought real life was brilliant. Now I felt like screaming at her, 'Don't tell me about real life. I know how bad it is.'

I woke up next morning and prayed it had all been a dream. Of course, it wasn't. And when I went to school I found it wasn't just my friends who were avoiding me. Everyone was – as if I had something catching. I had grassed on a friend. You can't sink any lower than that. Even Wizzie and her scummy mates knew that. Every time I passed them in the corridor they taunted me. Until finally, I couldn't take it any longer. I rammed Lauren against the wall before any of them could stop me. 'OK, maybe your sister didn't hear us, but one of the other waitresses did, and they told her.'

I'd had time to think about it and it was the only possible explanation. Grace and Sonya were on me in a second, dragging me off Lauren.

'Still can't admit you're a grass?' Grace sniggered. 'I hate cowards.'

I threw them off me. 'I'll find out who it was, don't you worry.'

'Who cares?' Wizzie sniggered. 'But say another word about Lauren's sister and you're in even more trouble, Driscoll.'

Lunchtime was the worst. I waited in the queue, alone, and with my tray in my hand I walked the length of the canteen to our table. We always sat at the same table. It was the Lip Gloss Girls' table and everyone knew it. No one else ever sat there. Our gang, our table and I automatically headed towards it. They saw me coming, didn't take their eyes off me. They waited till the last moment when I was right beside them before spreading themselves out, making it impossible for me to sit anywhere. I stood there for ages, like an idiot. I heard the sniggers all around, heard Wizzie's voice. 'It's not a tray she needs, it's a begging bowl.'

And still I couldn't move. 'Please,' I said, hating myself for sounding so pitiful. 'You're my best friends. Just let me sit down.'

Erin swore at me. I'd never heard her swear before. 'You're no friend of ours. Can you not take a hint?' And then she told me exactly where I could put my tray.

CHAPTER NINETEEN

My mother at last figured out something was wrong. Quick, eh? However, she thought it was a boy! 'First love,' she said. 'I remember mine. The ugliest boy in the school. I was mad about him, till somebody pointed out he was probably the best I could get. And I realised she was right. I was going with him because I couldn't get anybody better. Story of my life, eh?'

It wasn't going to be the story of mine! I'd always said I didn't want to be like my mother. I wasn't going to feel sorry for myself, or put myself down the way she did. Yet here I was, doing just that. I couldn't stop myself. I didn't even tell her it wasn't a boy. As if I'd be so upset over a boy! I just wanted her to go away.

Mrs Tasker saw how upset I was too. She kept me back in class, saw my red-rimmed eyes, saw how the others ignored me, passing me notebooks and pencils by their fingertips as if they might catch something off me.

'This has gone on far too long, Hannah.'

I knew she had heard the story and I wanted her to know I wasn't responsible. 'I'd never do anything like that.'

'Have you tried to talk to Erin on her own?'

'She won't listen. You see how none of them talk to me.'

She was silent for a moment, as if she was thinking about something. 'If I find a way for you to speak to her, do you think that would help?'

My heart leapt with hope. 'That's all I need, Mrs Tasker. If I had a chance to talk to Erin without other people butting in I know I could explain. She's my best friend.'

Mrs Tasker steered me towards the door. 'Come here at lunchtime, just before you're ready to go back to class. I'll have Erin here too.'

'She won't come if she knows I'm going to be here.'

'Then I won't tell her, Hannah. It'll be our secret.'

Our secret. The words were like a knife slicing through me now, but at least I had some hope. In the quiet of Mrs Tasker's classroom I would make Erin listen. Make her believe me. I knew I could.

All that morning I was like a cat on hot tiles. I couldn't stay still. Couldn't think of anything but meeting up with Erin.

I walked the corridor to Mrs Tasker's class as if I was a dead man walking. I was getting my chance and I wasn't going to waste it. If I could explain everything to Erin, then this would only be a hiccup in a perfect friendship.

Erin almost jumped out of the window when Mrs Tasker opened the door on me. Her face flushed with anger. 'So, this is why you wanted to see me. Well, I'm not staying. I don't want to talk to her.'

She got up from her seat but Mrs Tasker ordered her to sit down again, and Mrs Tasker is one of those teachers who, when she tells you to do something, you do it. She motioned me to the seat across from Erin.

'Now, I'll speak, and you will both listen,' she began. 'I've brought you here, because I see two girls who have always been friends. I've not always been happy about the direction that friendship was taking, but you were friends.'

'Not any more!' Erin snapped.

Mrs Tasker snapped back at her. 'You'll have your chance to speak, Erin.' Then she went on, 'Now, because one of you has inadvertently let something slip about the other . . .'

This time it was me who jumped to my feet. 'No. That's the whole point. I didn't let anything slip.'

'I'm sure it wasn't deliberate, Hannah,' Mrs Tasker said, as if she was making things better. But this wasn't what I wanted at all.

'Erin has to know that I didn't tell anyone. Honest.'

Erin tutted and sucked in her cheeks and looked out of the window.

Mrs Tasker only looked at me for a moment as if she was considering whether what I said could possibly be true. 'Well, that is something for Erin to think about too.' Yet I could see that she didn't believe me. I could see that in her eyes. She didn't blame me. She was sure it was accidentally done, but she had no doubt I had done it anyway. What chance did I have of convincing Erin?

'Why don't you speak to Erin now . . . have your say, and you, Erin, I want you to listen to all Hannah has to say without interrupting.'

I poured out my heart then, and Erin did listen. Her lips were pursed and her face was grim, but she listened. I spoke till I had nothing else to say, till I was just repeating the same thing over and over. 'It had to be someone else, Erin. Had to be.'

'But who?' Mrs Tasker asked.

My eyes flicked from Erin to the teacher, trying to convince them both. 'I thought at first it was Lauren's sister. She was a waitress at Erin's sister's wedding,' I explained.

'She's deaf,' Erin said flatly.

'I know, but what if one of the other waitresses overheard us and she told Lauren's sister. She could have used sign language or something. Then Lauren's sister tells Lauren and, zoom, it's all over the school by next day. That's the only explanation.'

Erin didn't say anything at first. She kept her eyes fixed on the floor. It was Mrs Tasker who spoke. 'Well, Erin, that seems a perfectly reasonable explanation. Hannah has sworn it wasn't her. Has she ever let you down before?'

Erin still didn't look at me, but she shook her head. 'No,' she said.

'Well, are you willing to shake hands on that?'

Erin still didn't say anything. I couldn't stop myself. 'Please, Erin, this has been horrible for me.'

'Horrible . . . for you?' Erin said, as if she was shocked.

'Horrible for you too, I know that.'

Mrs Tasker leant over and touched Erin's hand. 'Come on, Erin. Think of all the good times you've had together. All the years of friendship you've shared.'

Erin looked at me at last. I couldn't fathom her eyes. She held my gaze for a long time before turning to our teacher. 'All right,' she said. Her voice was barely a whisper.

It was as if the sun had burst into the office. 'All right.' Magic words. My hand was shaking as I held it out to her. Mrs Tasker nodded and smiled. 'Go on, Erin.'

Erin took my hand. Hers was cold and clammy and limp. I shook it so hard I thought it would fall off. 'Oh, thanks, Erin. Thanks. You won't be sorry. I'll be the best friend you ever had from now on.'

I knew I was on the verge of tears, felt them welling up in my eyes. But I didn't want to cry. I was too happy to cry.

Mrs Tasker stood up and sighed. A job well done. 'Now, you two girls run along to class. I told your teacher you'd both be a little late.'

She stood at her classroom door watching us as we walked off, side by side. I couldn't stop babbling. 'Oh

Erin, everything's going to be so good now. You'll see. We'll get Lauren back for it, don't you worry.'

Erin stopped walking and turned to me. She glanced at Mrs Tasker's door. It was just closing. Erin's face twisted into an ugly grin. 'Did you really think I believed any of the crap you were spouting in there?'

I reached out to touch her arm and she drew herself back as if I was a leper. 'You must think my head buttons up at the back, Driscoll. Because I am no friend of yours and never will be again.' Then she leant close to my face. 'And we are going to get you for this. Don't you worry. We're going to make you sorry.'

And then she was gone, clattering down the corridor at full speed. And I knew then it was no use. I was no longer her friend. Never would be again.

It was over.

PART TWO

LIMBO

CHAPTER TWENTY

The days seemed to merge into a nightmare – a nightmare I never seemed to wake from. I was literally without friends. I had never needed any others except for the Lip Gloss Girls – hadn't bothered making any. In fact, I'd shunned most of the other girls. We all had. They weren't good enough for any of us. Now they were all getting their own back on me. They shunned me.

'Don't try to be our pal now, Driscoll,' I would be told. 'We don't want Erin's cast-offs.'

That was the message whenever I tried to be friendly with anyone. I was Erin's cast-off and nobody wanted me. I would stand silently in a corner of the yard and watch as they passed me by.

I would see Wizzie and the rest forward their text messages about me from one phone to another, giggling at me, laughing out loud at whatever was written. I was a joke. And I had no answer for them.

'Where's your smart mouth now?' someone asked me one day. Yes, where was my smart mouth? I couldn't find the joke in this at all. Didn't know how to handle it.

I was pushed and jostled in the corridors, left to sit alone in the canteen. Always alone.

'How does it feel to be bullied yourself?' Nan Gates, one of the other girls in my class, asked me one day.

'I was never a bully!' I said to her. Yet I remembered the times we had made fun of her frizzy red hair, called her a 'ginger', rejected her attempts to be one of us. Had I been a bully?

How I hated going to school. I made futile excuses to stay home. They seldom worked. Mrs Tasker watched me closely. She knew her little ploy hadn't worked, but she didn't try again. I couldn't blame her. It would have been no use. There was nothing left. It was as if me and the rest of the girls had never been friends.

Mum asked why my friends never came round to visit any more. Why was I never round at Erin's? Why didn't they phone? I made excuse after excuse. I became an expert at lying.

'We're all studying hard.'

'Heather's been grounded.'

'Erin has flu.'

I even took to going to the cinema myself, and pretended I was meeting the girls there. Sad, or what?

One awful night I was sitting in the back row when they all came in, Erin and Rose and Heather. They were giggling, chucking popcorn at each other and everyone else, making too much noise, talking too loud. I slid so far down in my seat I was practically on the floor, terrified they would spot me – see how pathetic I'd become. And yet, I couldn't bring myself to leave. I was mesmerised watching them, wishing I was still one of them, still sharing all that fun.

I wondered if they ever missed me too. Missed my jokes. Missed all the fun we'd had together. I watched them for ages in the dark of the cinema, then I snuck out, almost crawling on my hands and knees. Crawling like a dog. Ridiculous, and funny too. Even I could see the funny side of it.

That night I cried myself to sleep. I hated myself for being such a wimp. I wanted to be angry at them, but I couldn't. It was me I was angry at, always feeling sorry for myself, drowning myself in misery.

Next morning, I came to a decision. I would make

one last-ditch attempt to explain things to Erin. What did I have to lose? I was going to write her a letter. She couldn't erase a letter. Surely, she would be intrigued enough to read what I had to say?

It was Sunday. Mum went off to Mass without her usual Sunday morning moan because I didn't go with her. 'I think you're coming down with something, Hannah,' she said, feeling my brow. 'You haven't been yourself for days.'

I sat at my window and watched the people on the quiet streets heading for church. Or going off to do some Sunday shopping.

Sunday had always been the Lip Gloss Girls' day out. Going to the café on the quay, then walking back and forth along the waterfront, arm in arm, making people step off the pavement to pass us. And here I was, alone, trying to compose a letter that would make them want to walk arm in arm with me again.

I thought about it for a long time. It had to be just the right kind of letter. Then it came to me. I'd be funny, the way they always liked me to be. Funny Hannah. I'd write a letter that would make them laugh, make them giggle. I would write such a funny letter it would make them all laugh out loud. 'Trust Hannah,' I could almost hear Erin say it. 'I'd forgotten how funny she could be.' And they would realise how much they missed me.

That was it. I would make them laugh.

CHAPTER TWENTY-ONE

I sat up all night composing that letter – ripping out pages, crumpling them and chucking them into the wastepaper basket. I had to find exactly the right words. Funny, cheeky and yet . . . apologetic. (Though I knew I had done nothing wrong, by this time I would apologise for anything they wanted.) I wanted us to start again, go back to square one.

The letter would be addressed to Erin. She was the one who had been hurt . . . though not by me. In my head I kept thinking that if I did this right, by next week all that had happened would be a horrible memory, nothing more.

Mum came into my room at midnight, demanding I put the light out. 'Just finishing my homework,' I told her.

It was hours later before I was done, before I was satisfied. I slipped the letter in an envelope. Should I post it? If I posted it she wouldn't get it until the next day – so I decided against that. Speed was of the essence. I wanted Erin to get that letter today, Monday. I wanted her to read it. I wanted to put all this behind me.

On a Monday, we had PE, period one, straight after assembly. Erin always hung her blazer on the same hook. I decided that I would slip the letter into her pocket when no one was looking. Surely curiosity alone would make her read it. And once she'd read it, she had to feel something of our old friendship?

I hardly slept and went to school looking like something out of a zombie movie. The letter shook in my hand as I pushed it into the pocket of Erin's blazer. I was terrified someone might catch me, assume I was taking something out instead. That was all I needed now, to be accused of stealing.

I could hardly bear to glance over to Erin as we changed after the lesson, expecting every time her hand went into her pocket that she would find the letter and pluck it out. But she didn't. Not then. She giggled and whispered with Heather and Rose as they hovered around her like a cloaking device, protecting her from me. Then they were gone. The door banged shut and I was left alone in the changing rooms.

In our next lesson too it was obvious she hadn't read it – either that or she was a very good actress. But no, she hadn't read it. I would have known if she had. Didn't I know her better than anyone? Wasn't she my best friend?

But by the time I walked into the school canteen at lunchtime I knew she'd found it and read it. I knew by the way they all turned and stared at me as I carried my tray up the canteen, looking for a table. I think I stopped breathing as I felt their eyes on me. As I came close, Erin, sitting on the edge of the table, plucked the letter from her pocket and held it out to me.

I nodded, attempting a smile. A 'yes, it was me,' kind of smile.

And Erin smiled back.

I almost dropped my tray. It had worked. When Erin beckoned me over to her, I almost ran.

'You sent me this?'

I was nodding like one of those dogs you see in the back of cars. 'Uhh, it was the only way I could let you know how I . . .'

She stopped me gabbling, holding up her hand in front of my face in that bossy way Erin had. 'You have to hear this, girls.'

I realised then that they had all gathered round me. Did that mean I was back in the fold again? Or were they hemming me in so I couldn't move? I wasn't sure.

'This is *so* sweet,' Erin said, and she flicked the pages of the letter and began to read it aloud.

'My dear friend, Erin. And you are my friend. Always will be.'

I tried to interrupt her. I didn't want her to read it like this, here in the school canteen. But I couldn't stop her now.

'How long has it been now? A week, two? Too long anyway. What are you like, Erin?

Monday: Out with my best friend, Hannah.

Tuesday: Blame Hannah for something she didn't do.

Wednesday: Wash my hair.

Thursday: Joke over. Bored without her. She's such a great laugh. How could I ever have blamed Hannah for anything?'

Erin looked round at everyone. 'See what she's doing? She's writing it like a diary. Bridget blinkin' Jones diary! Isn't that clever?'

There was a murmured giggle. I looked round them. I was smiling too. 'You know me,' I said.

'There's more,' Erin said, and she began to read on. Only this time her voice changed, from giggling as if she was enjoying it, to sad and pathetic. Not the way I had meant it to be read at all. Turning the meaning upside down.

'*Monday: Found Hannah's letter in my pocket. Couldn't stop laughing as I read it. She is so funny. I miss her so much.*' Erin looked up at everyone again and pretended to sob. 'Boo – hoo!' Then she went on, '*Only Hannah could think of a way like this to apologise. (Though she didn't do anything. Not guilty, ma'am.)*

Monday night: Talk all this over with the girls. Rose, who's going to be great in the school show, by the way – talk about boot licking!' Erin giggled.

I tried to snatch the letter from her hand but she turned away. I couldn't even run, trapped by the crowd.

'Oh, listen to this. This is classic: *Heather's so understanding. "We just don't have the same laughs without Hannah," Heather says. We all decide to call Hannah at once. She's waiting for that call. Skips over to my place on a high. Hugs and kisses and my mum's ice cream all round and she's dying to see the wedding photos! The Lip Gloss Girls together again. For ever!*' Erin burst out laughing. 'Doesn't that make you cry?' But the laugh died on her lips when she turned to me. 'Do you really think that's how it will happen?'

I knew it wouldn't. Not now. I'd been an idiot to think this would work. I felt as if there was a lead weight in my stomach. I watched, everyone did, as Erin very slowly tore my letter in half. 'You're pathetic.'

'Sad little girl,' Heather said.

'Loser,' said Rose.

I was suddenly shoved so hard my tray slipped from my hands. My dinner – cottage pie, rhubarb and custard – went everywhere. They all jumped back. 'And clumsy too,' Erin said.

I was ready to cry. Why couldn't I stop myself from crying? I hated myself for it. 'What is it you want from me? What do I have to do?'

Erin slid down from the table. 'What do you have to do? Let me see . . . Keep well back from all of us from now on . . . that's all. We'll know when you're too close.' She pinched her nose. 'Smells awful.'

In another life, when I was another Hannah, I would have answered that. 'Then you must have peed your knickers again, Erin!' But I couldn't hurt her like that. Why couldn't I hurt her when she was hurting me so much?

'You're the saddest thing I've ever seen,' Heather said, as she passed me. 'Trying to get round us with that pathetic attempt at a letter.'

And one by one they stepped past me, stamping my 'pathetic attempt at a letter' into the floor along with my cottage pie. I was left alone. Completely alone.

CHAPTER TWENTY-TWO

I stood there like an idiot, cottage pie all over my shoes. When I looked around, there was Wizzie and her gang, grinning at me. I found my voice at last. 'What are you gawping at?' I yelled at them.

It was Sonya who answered. Sonya with her stutter.

'S-s-somebody nobody likes.'

Once I would have snapped back at her, made a fool of her. Now I couldn't think of anything to say. She was right. I was someone nobody liked. It was so unfair. In a few days I had gone from Hannah, always surrounded by friends, to Driscoll, the girl who was constantly alone.

Zak Riley was at the door of the canteen when I stumbled through, as if him and his mates were waiting for me. 'I'd hate to be a lassie,' he said.

'You're too much of a wimp. We'd never have you.' A little of the old Hannah coming through. Why couldn't it come through when I spoke to Erin?

That night at home, I couldn't hold back any tears. I cried so much I eventually made myself sick. I had to run from my room and just made it to the bathroom in time. I hung over the toilet, retching. It reminded me of the night of the wedding, and made me cry all the more.

Mum came pounding on the door. 'Hannah! What's up with you?'

I came out, my face drained of any colour, beads of sweat dotting my brow. Mum looked almost as bad. Face grey, her eyes wide with alarm. 'Hannah, what's wrong with you?'

And finally, it all came pouring out. I told her everything. The only thing I didn't tell her was Erin's secret. Loyal to the last.

Mum listened and when I'd finished she slumped against the back of her chair. 'Oh, Hannah, thank goodness.'

Thank goodness?! I almost yelled at her then, but she added, 'I thought you were going to tell me you were pregnant.'

The old me would have laughed herself silly at that. Me? No boyfriend, and no interest in any either. I might still have laughed, we might both have, if she hadn't gone on to say, 'That would be just my luck. You getting pregnant at your age.'

Suddenly, it was all about Mum again and her hard luck. It made me so angry. 'Oh well, we can't have you having any bad luck, can we? We'll not worry about what's happening to me.'

She looked taken aback. Then she had the cheek to say, 'Everything has to be about you, hasn't it? What did you do to bring this about, eh?'

'Have you not been listening, Mum? I didn't do anything.'

'Have you apologised?'

'Apologised for what?' Why didn't she ever listen? 'I didn't do anything.'

'So how come they're not talking to you?' She didn't wait for an answer. 'I saw this coming. That lot think you're not good enough for them, eh? That Erin's mother thinks she's something. She always thought she was better than me. She's always been luckier, that's all. Everything fell into her lap. She married a man with a good job, and what did I get? Your dad. A real loser. Oh well, like attracts like. But that's how that Erin's so stuck up. She thinks she's better than you as well.'

She ranted on and on, and I was forgotten. It was her bad luck. She patted my shoulders and turned down my

126

bed like a good mother, but all the time she only made me feel worse. We were both losers, that was her message. She was like a broken record.

I lay in the dark and tried to sleep, but my mind was too filled with all that had happened today. The humiliation of Erin reading out my letter in front of everyone. It played over and over in my head like a scene from a horror movie.

It was my mum's raised voice that brought me out of the nightmare. I sat up in bed, wondering who she was shouting at. But there was no other voice. Only hers. She was on the phone, and as I listened, her voice grew louder, her tone more strident.

And suddenly I knew who she was yelling at. Erin's mother. She was on the phone to Erin's mother. I felt like being sick again. What did she think she was doing?

I leapt out of bed.

'So you think your daughter can treat my daughter like that? Well, you can think again.' She paused and I knew Erin's mother was talking to her, shouting at her in fact, though I couldn't hear what she was saying. Whatever it was it was making Mum even more angry. 'What did you call me? You take that back. Don't you dare say that about me!'

She was almost losing it. I tried to pull the phone out of her hands, but she yanked it away from me, kept on shouting down the line. 'And as for your daughter, Hannah's told me all about her. She's got no reason to be such a snob. She deserves everything she gets!' I could hear the click on the line. 'Hello!' Mum screamed. 'Don't you dare hang up on me!' She shook the phone as if she expected Erin's mother to drop out of the receiver.

Finally, I managed to pull it from her. 'What have you done?!'

She was shaking with anger. 'I was trying to help. I thought I could talk to that woman, but she is such a snob. Thinks she is something.'

'You said I told you all about Erin.'

She shrugged that off as if she thought it wasn't important. 'You say a lot of things when you're angry.' Then she walked off into the kitchen. 'I need a cup of tea . . . I can't get over what that woman said to me!'

It was bad enough Mum had phoned Erin's house, but she had said that I had told her all about Erin, as if I had told her Erin's secret too.

Now I had no hope of convincing anyone otherwise.

CHAPTER TWENTY-THREE

It couldn't get any worse, I thought, but I was wrong. Next day I discovered just how bad it could get. As soon as I walked through the school gates I knew they were going to start on me. They were all gathered round Erin and when she saw me she whispered something in Rose's ear. And suddenly they all looked at me and laughed.

'Her mother said *what*?!' Rose shouted in a dramatic voice. Always said she should be an actress. They all knew exactly what my mother had said. It had been well rehearsed.

'Like mother, like daughter,' Erin sneered. 'That's what my mum says. Her mother's always been over the top about everything. Can't handle life, my mum says.'

'Can't handle a boil on the backside, my mum says.' This was Heather, and she turned on me and her eyes were dark with venom. 'She'll go the same way as her

129

mother, my mum says.' And I knew what she meant. They all did. No secret about my mum.

'Sooner the better,' Rose said, and my eyes filled up with tears. How could they be so cruel? I should have had a smart answer for them. I should have been sticking up for my mother. Instead, I wanted to agree with them – anything to make them my friends again. After last night, my mum had only made things worse for me. I ran from them into the school building, trying to block out their catcalls behind me.

It was during the first lesson that the police arrived. We could all see the car from the class window as it pulled to a halt. Two officers, a man and a woman, strode towards the main entrance. I saw Wizzie exchange a look with Sonya, and I remembered the old woman who had been held up in the town. Good. They had been caught at last.

It was only a short time later that Wizzie, Sonya, Grace and Lauren were being summoned out of our class. They all swaggered as if they had nothing to fear, daring us to say a word. Someone dared. Rose. As they passed her desk she whispered, 'Scumbags!' and Lauren glared at her.

A buzz went round the class as soon as they'd gone. I wasn't part of that buzz. I had no one to buzz with now.

Mrs Tasker slapped a book on her desk to shut us up, and though the lesson continued, nobody really listened. All we could think of was Wizzie and her gang and what was happening in the office.

'They've probably been arrested,' I said to no one in particular as we pushed our way out of class. Just as well, as no one in particular answered me.

They didn't appear again till lunchtime, striding into the school yard, laughing and looking as if they'd got away with murder, one up on the police. I hated them in that moment. I thought of the old lady and the photo of her I'd seen in the papers, upset and vulnerable, and I hated them for it.

I wasn't the only one.

'I can't believe you're laughing!' Heather snapped at the Hell Cats as they passed her.

'Believe it!' Lauren said, squaring up to her.

'What business is it of yours, anyway?' Grace came up behind Lauren, her big horsey face angry.

'She thinks we're scum,' Wizzie said.

Rose spat on the ground. 'You are scum. Always were and always will be.'

I thought there would be a fight then. I waited for Wizzie to launch herself at Rose, or one of the others. She would have too, I was sure of it. But just at that moment one of the teachers appeared. He stood at the main door, glaring directly at Wizzie, and behind him the two police officers stepped from the building and stopped. Their cold stare was aimed at Wizzie too. They knew the Hell Cats were guilty, I was sure of it – just didn't have enough evidence to prove it.

The police headed for their car and left. Wizzie waited till they were gone. Then she leant close to Rose. 'Catch you later for that,' Wizzie mouthed, and I knew there was trouble coming. The first time there would be trouble and I wouldn't be there to share it. I'd always known my boldness gave them courage. How could they manage without me? Maybe they wouldn't want to.

Or maybe I had another chance to show them they needed me.

'Catch you later,' Wizzie had warned. And I was going to be there when she did.

CHAPTER TWENTY-FOUR

Wizzie and her gang never wasted any time. If they said they would catch you later, you'd better be ready for later to mean later that same day. I knew that, so I hung around the gates waiting to see what would happen.

They were standing by the bus stop, watching for Erin and Rose and Heather coming out of the school gates. Cameron High stands at the top of the hill, overlooking the town. Beyond the school there is a sprawling new estate of modern houses, but go past that estate and you are into the wilds of nowhere.

When I saw Wizzie and her gang standing by that bus stop, silhouetted against the darkening sky, it sent a shiver down the back of my neck. I wasn't afraid. As I watched my friends – why did I still call them my friends? – as I watched them strolling out of the school gates I knew how they would be feeling. Tensed and ready for anything. My eyes darted to Wizzie and the others, spread out across the street. Grace stood with her fists clenched and she'd never looked more like a horse – a war horse. Lauren kept licking her lips nervously. Then there was Wizzie, bold and scary – that knife of hers was never far from everyone's mind. Though I'd never known her to use it. But get Wizzie, and once she was out of action the rest would fall like pins in a bowling alley. But my friends didn't have me there to whisper that advice to them. Instead, they had Geraldine Mooney, standing beside them where I should be. I'd been replaced already.

Common sense told me to go home and forget about them. Let them get on with it themselves. I shouldn't care. But I couldn't move. It was as if my feet were glued to the ground.

They stopped and stared at the Hell Cats.

'What are you looking at?' Grace said, and at the same time she moved forward. And suddenly, it was Mooney who leapt towards her – showing off if you ask me, desperate to make an impression. She landed against Grace and bounced off her. I could have told her she would have done that. She fell back on the ground and Grace laughed that neighing laugh of hers and stepped over her. By that time they were all on each other. Wizzie grunted and grabbed at Heather. Heather screamed as Wizzie gripped her hair and lifted her from the ground. Erin and Rose had jumped in too and suddenly they were all a mass of arms and legs, flailing about wildly.

Erin was on the ground, struggling to get up, but big Grace was almost sitting on her. Mooney was trying to pull her off, but she had Lauren attached to her neck.

They were losing. My friends were losing. They needed me. They must see that. I couldn't help myself. I didn't even think about it really. I didn't do it to impress or even to get back in with them. It came as naturally as flicking a fly from my face. I jumped in to help them.

I had Lauren off Geraldine in a moment and landed a punch that sent her reeling across the ground. I pushed Geraldine aside and gave Grace such a ferocious push she went toppling off Erin. I reached for Erin's hand and pulled her to her feet. Her eyes flashed when she saw me, but I turned from her till we were standing, back to back, the way we always did. Ready to take on all comers. I was swaying on my feet as Grace headed back towards me. I stretched out my arms, eager to take her on. The adrenalin rushed through me.

And suddenly, Grace stopped in her tracks. In fact,

everything stopped. It was like that bit in a movie when the soundtrack fades and the action goes into slow motion. I felt a hand on my shoulder. I turned, ready to punch, thinking it was Wizzie or one of the others who had grabbed me.

But it was Erin. Her face was angry, her voice bitter. 'Piss off!' she said. 'We don't need any help from you.'

'But . . .' I looked round them and I'll never forget the triumph on Wizzie's face.

She dusted herself off. 'Yeah, let's put this off till another day. You lot aren't able to handle us on your own.'

And I realised that was what I had done. I had made it look as if the Lip Gloss Girls couldn't win a fight without me.

'Erin, I didn't mean . . . I only wanted . . .'

None of them listened. Erin spat on the ground in front of me. 'I wish you could take the hint . . . You're not wanted.'

'Aye, it takes a while for her to get a message, doesn't it?' This was Wizzie. She popped the chewing gum she had stuck behind her ear back in her mouth. 'No longer welcome. Even I can read that one.'

Heather helped Geraldine to her feet. 'Good going,

Gerry,' she said. 'We would have won if that git hadn't interfered.'

In your dreams, I wanted to say. Why couldn't I?

They all moved off, until only Wizzie was left, standing across from me, chewing her gum, sneering at me.

'All alone, eh, Driscoll? Och, don't cry. You won't be alone for long . . . cos one dark night me and the lassies'll get you and show you just what being alone means . . .'

And she swaggered off and left me. Alone. And for the first time, scared.

CHAPTER TWENTY-FIVE

Why couldn't I stop crying? Why was I so miserable? Every afternoon I'd go home from school and try to eat my dinner, though every morsel stuck in my throat. Half the time I threw it all up later. I'd go into my room and try to concentrate on my homework. But it would bring back memories of how homework was always interrupted by phone calls and texts between us all. The phone never rang now. No one called me. I tried to pretend it didn't matter. I'd go to bed and pull the covers over my head and hope when I woke up everything would have changed back.

I had turned into a different person. Where was the old Hannah, the one I could rely on? I waited to hear her voice deep within me, whispering to me, *Who needs them? You can manage without them.* But she had deserted me along with my friends. Friends! I didn't have any friends any more.

Feeling sorry for me?

Don't bother. I was feeling sorry enough for myself. Every night I'd end up crying. No matter what I did to try and stop myself. Putting on my favourite comedy video only seemed to make things worse. I remembered how Heather had bought it for my birthday. Reading a funny book, I couldn't even see the words through my tears. Finally, I'd give up, get into bed and just cry myself to sleep.

Perhaps it would have helped if I'd had brothers or sisters. This would never have happened to Erin with her protective family brood surrounding her. Big brother teasing her, her sisters spending time with her to take her mind off it.

But I had no one. Not even a favourite aunt to confide in. My mother and her sister didn't talk any more. They'd been 'estranged' for years. 'Estranged' was one of my mother's favourite words. She used it so often. She was 'estranged' from most people. And that made me wonder if it ran in the family, this knack of losing friends, becoming 'estranged'. Was I my mother's daughter? I hoped not. I didn't want to be like my mother.

My mind was in a constant turmoil, thinking all the

time. It was because I had no one to talk to. No one except my mother, and I didn't want to talk to her. In a weak moment I told her about the fight outside school, about Wizzie's threat. She almost hit the roof, and I shut her up by telling her that Wizzie had started another fight with someone else and had forgotten about me.

Yet I knew she was worried about me. She never stopped asking me about what was happening at school, watching for my answer, knowing I was lying when I'd tell her everything was fine.

One night, she came into my room. She looked as if she'd been crying too. 'This just can't go on, Hannah,' she said. 'Every night you're stuck in this room. You sleep half the time. You don't go out any more. I don't know how to help you if you don't talk to me.'

How could I talk to her? The last time I'd confided in her she'd gone on the phone to Erin's mother. I couldn't risk that again.

'I'll be fine,' I said. 'I just need time.'

She sat on the bed. Did I look like her? I wondered. I'd never thought so, but now as I caught a glimpse of us together in my mirrored wardrobe, our hair messy, our faces streaked with tears, I saw a distinct resemblance.

Like mother, like daughter.

I didn't want to be like my mother.

'I've been thinking a lot about this, Hannah.' She pushed back her hair the way she always did when she was nervous. 'What do you think about changing schools?'

Changing schools. I hadn't considered that at all. Starting afresh, making a new set of friends. For the first time in ages I felt my heart lift. I could change schools, pretend none of this had ever happened. And then my mother said something that made me realise I could never do it.

'That's what I would do in your position. Just move away, leave it all behind you.'

That's what my mum would do. Run away. I felt she always ran away from her problems, never faced up to them. And I wasn't going to be like her.

'I like my school, Mum,' I said. 'Why should I be the one to run away? Let them change schools if they want. I'm not going to.'

I tried to make it sound light-hearted, but my mum didn't take it that way. She stood up and began pacing

141

the room. 'That school you like so much has done nothing to help you. You're going through all this and they just sit on their backsides and do nothing. What about this anti-bullying policy they're supposed to have?'

'I'm not being bullied, Mum,' I tried to tell her, because I wasn't. I was being frozen out by my friends, and ignored by everyone else. But I wasn't being bullied. She wouldn't listen.

'These things are going on right under their noses and they do nothing to help. Oh yes, they want all the kudos for being teachers, but they don't want any of the responsibility.'

She was talking rubbish. 'It's not the teachers' fault, Mum.' But still she wouldn't listen. She went on and on, as if she was thinking aloud, venting all her pent-up anger on the teachers, on the school. Finally, I couldn't listen any more. 'Shut up, please, Mum, just shut up!'

Her face tightened with anger. 'I'm trying to be on your side. Isn't that what you want?'

'Well, think of another way to be on my side, OK!'

She slammed out of the room and I thought I had shut her up. But I was wrong.

She took me at my word. She thought of another way to be on my side. Next day she did the very worst thing she could.

She came to the school.

CHAPTER TWENTY-SIX

I was in English when the teacher called me out of the class. Her face was so stern I knew something was wrong. Anne O'Donnell had been called out one day by a teacher wearing this same expression, to be told her father had been killed in an accident. So as I followed her along the corridor, I was expecting the worst. But not this.

My mother was sitting in Mr McGinty's office. So was Mrs Tasker, standing beside the headmaster, looking as grim as he was.

Mum had been crying. She was blowing her nose and her face was almost hidden by a cloud of tissues. Her eyes, all I could see, were puffy with tears. My heart sank like a stone when I saw her. What was she doing here?

'Sit down, Hannah,' Mr McGinty ordered me.

I took the seat beside my mother, but when she

stretched out her hand to touch mine I shrank from her.

'What's happened?' I asked.

'Your mother's very worried about you, it would seem.' The head's voice was cold and I knew he wasn't impressed by my mother's attitude. 'She seems to think you're going through a major trauma and that we are doing nothing to help. Is that true?'

I glared at my mother. She looked back at me innocently. 'I told them everything, Hannah. The way that crowd are treating you is disgraceful. You're home every night on your own, crying.' She looked back at the headmaster. 'They all turned on her the other day during a fight outside the school.'

Mr McGinty almost leapt out of his chair. 'Is this true?'

I didn't know how to answer that. Deny it and make my mother out to be a liar? Or admit it and do the worst thing you can ever do – grass? In the end, I said nothing. I bit my lip and stared at the floor. I didn't have to say a word anyway. My mother did all the talking. I couldn't have shut her up with anaesthetic.

'And now one of the other gangs is threatening her – her with the funny name and everything pierced. She told her they're going to get her.'

Why couldn't she ever keep her mouth shut? I bit my lip even harder to keep from screaming.

'She's terrified to come to school. And you do nothing to protect her. I'll go to the authorities. I'll go to the papers. I'll do something about it if you won't.'

My mother's voice was becoming almost hysterical.

She was making me sound like the world's biggest wimp. 'I am not terrified,' I said at last, trying to keep my voice calm. I didn't want to sound like my mum. 'I've fallen out with my friends, that's all.'

'I tried to help the girls to make up,' Mrs Tasker said.

I shrugged my shoulders. 'It didn't last. Doesn't matter. I've got other friends.'

'She hasn't!' my mother shouted. That really made me feel worse. 'She's got no one. They've all deserted her.'

It took all my willpower not to cry. She was making me sound like the biggest kind of loser.

'Mrs Driscoll,' the head said when he could get a word in edgeways. 'I don't like the gang culture in this school. Especially amongst the girls.'

'They're worse than boys,' my mother said loudly.

Worse than boys. How chuffed I had once been to be told that.

'We intend to do something about it. As for Hannah being bullied –'

'I'm not being bullied –' I tried to tell them but he wouldn't let me finish.

'We will be dealing with that too.' Mr McGinty looked at me then. 'I don't ever want you to be afraid to come to school, or afraid while you are here. But you have to let us know what's happening. As for this fight, I'm not going to let this pass without a word. And if anyone is threatening you they are going to be in big trouble.'

I wanted to plead with him to forget my mother had ever been here. But I knew it was too late. Wheels had been set in motion and things were going to get worse.

CHAPTER TWENTY-SEVEN

I stormed from the office without even looking at my mum. She tried to touch me, to pull me round to face her, and I jerked myself away from her angrily.

'I'm only trying to help,' she said.

How could she possibly think this was helping?

Everyone knew she'd come to the school. Lots of people had seen her barging in and demanding to see the headmaster. The word had gone round the school like a bushfire in a drought.

At break they were all round me in the yard. 'See if you've got us into any trouble, Driscoll,' Rose pushed herself against me, 'you're going to get it.'

'I haven't . . . I didn't.'

'So, what was your mother doing here?'

I tried to think of an answer, but my hesitation was answer enough.

'Have you got to tell your mother everything?'

'Leave her be,' Erin said with a sneer that didn't flatter her. 'Her mother's as useless as she is.'

And suddenly, Mrs Tasker was there, pulling me from them. It was as if she'd been sent there to look after me, to save me from them.

'I want to see all of you immediately after break. In Mr McGinty's office.' Then she looked at me. 'You can come with me, Hannah.'

I could hear them snigger as I walked off, safe with the teacher.

It wasn't only Erin and the others who were summoned to the head's office. Wizzie and her mates were there too.

They were all there when I walked in with Mrs Tasker. Every one of them glared at me, blaming me, and I couldn't argue with that. I would have blamed me too. Blamed my mum.

Everyone else had to stand. Only I was allowed to sit down, beside the teacher. It was humiliating. Out of the corner of my eye I could see Wizzie lean back against the wall. Grace was biting at her nails and Lauren was sighing noisily as if she was bored stiff. Erin was standing as straight as if a board was rammed up her back. There was anger in the way she stood. Anger at me.

Heather was drumming her fingers on the head's desk, a daring deed for Heather. Mr McGinty brought a ruler sharply down on the desk inches from Heather's hand. She jumped and Sonya giggled.

'I believe there was a fight outside the school the other day.' I must have looked guilty. No one would ever believe now that I wasn't the one who grassed. 'Well, the school won't have it. We won't put up with these fights any more. We've had enough visits from the police to last a lifetime.' His gaze went directly to Wizzie. 'People have been hurt.'

Wizzie shrugged her shoulders. 'Wasn't us,' she said.

Mr McGinty roared at her. 'Don't you dare talk back to me! A bunch of silly little girls acting like the mafia, causing nothing but trouble. Not caring who they hurt? I don't understand your mentality.' He looked directly at Heather. 'Why are you in a gang, Heather?'

Heather pursed her lips and looked sweet. 'I'm not in a gang, sir. I just go about with my friends.'

'And what about you, Wizzie? Why are you in a gang?'

'I'm not in a gang either. Better ask the Lip Gloss Girls about going into gangs.'

'Do you get a kick out of everyone doing what you say?'

Wizzie laughed. 'Nobody ever listens to me, sir.' She nudged Sonya. 'That right, Sonya?'

Sonya pretended she hadn't heard. 'Did somebody say something there?'

That set them all laughing, but it only made the head even angrier. 'I can't understand you. You get yourselves into these stupid gangs and then you can turn on a friend just like that.' He snapped his fingers. Everyone knew he meant me. If I'd had the nerve I would have crawled out of the room.

'This is the final warning. I'm going to be watching all of you from now on. And I'm going to be speaking to all of your parents.'

Mrs Tasker held me back until everyone else had left the room. I wondered if she could feel my shoulders shaking under her hand. Now I was really in trouble. Couldn't they see that? Where was it all going to end? How was it all going to end?

I was ignored by them all until home time. I was desperate to get out of the school gates, away from everything. Though I knew home and my mum were no comfort to me. I expected Erin and the rest to be waiting for me, but it was Wizzie who was there. She wasn't even looking at me when she spoke. She spoke in a voice so soft that anyone looking might have thought she hadn't even noticed I was there. But her words were just like a knife inside me.

'You're going to be really sorry for grassing us up, Driscoll. One dark night, me and the girls are coming to get you. And you'll have nobody to back you up.'

Then she moved inches closer so I could catch her next words. 'See, McGinty had it all wrong. Being in a gang means you belong. And you, Driscoll, don't belong any more.'

CHAPTER TWENTY-EIGHT

It was true. I didn't belong any more. And every day after that, I could feel Wizzie and her gang watching me. They were going to get me for grassing, and I remembered all the times we'd come up against each other. I hadn't been afraid then, but I'd always had my gang to back me up. Now I had no one.

It wasn't that everyone turned against me. Moira Hood, in my class, a really nice girl, always asked me to sit with her in the canteen, came to talk to me in the yard. But they even managed to turn that against me.

'I see you're Moira's latest charity case,' Erin muttered one day as she passed me in the corridor.

A charity case, that's exactly what I felt like.

Zak Riley offered to let me join his crowd. 'You're safer with a bunch of boys, Hannah.' And that made all his friends laugh. If I'd thought he was serious I might just have agreed.

I met Rose's brother coming out of the boys' toilets one day and hurried after him. Rose thinks her brother's brilliant and I thought that maybe if I could talk to him he would pass a message on to Rose.

I called after him and he turned round. I saw his eyes go up in exasperation. 'What is it, Hannah?'

'I want you to talk to Rose.'

'I already have. I think you're all acting like idiots. But girls fall out all the time. It's not the end of the world, Hannah.'

I realised then that what was the end of the world for me, was to him just his sister and one of her pals having a falling out. He saw how pale my face was. How could he not?

'Don't let it get to you,' he said. 'You look ill.'

In a way, I was ill. I was sick to my stomach all the time. Because I cry myself to sleep every night, I wanted to tell him, but he answered it himself. 'There's a bug going about. Think you might have caught it.' Then he took another step back as if he might catch it too.

He left, assuring me he would talk to his sister. I think he only said that to get away from me. When I turned from him, there were Wizzie and Grace and Lauren all watching and smirking. I felt even sicker.

My only hope was that it just might work. Rose thought the world of her big brother. Maybe she'd listen to him.

Everyone in school was aware that Wizzie and her gang had threatened to get me. Most people thought I had it coming – hadn't I always been fighting with them? Moira thought I should tell one of the teachers. In Moira's world, the teachers always helped. But I was done with teachers.

It was later that same day when Rose passed a note to me. For a moment, a wonderful moment, I thought I had the answer I was looking for. She even smiled, with those bright white teeth of hers she was so proud of. Teeth that didn't need the brace everyone else wore. My hands were shaking as I unfolded it.

Don't ever speak to my brother again. You deserve everything you get. Grass.

I looked back at her and her smile had turned to a snarl. Erin and the rest erupted with laughter. She'd told them all.

The teacher turned from the blackboard. 'What's the joke?' he snapped.

And Erin mouthed to me, 'You are.'

Wizzie saw it all. Her gaze seemed to say, 'No one to

back you up. Not long now.' It was as if she was playing with me, the way a cat plays with a mouse, waiting for the right moment to pounce on me. And I couldn't get Wizzie's knife out of my head. She'd never used it in a fight with us. In fact, I'd never even seen her with one. But it was all I thought about. She'd never use it on me, would she? But I had heard on the news just that morning, about a girl who had been stabbed in the school dinner queue because she'd grassed.

Even then my humiliation wasn't over. I was scared to go out of the school gates that day, sure they would be waiting for me. If there had been another exit I would have used it. Erin and Heather hung back too.

'What's the problem, Hannah? Scared the Hell Cats are gonny get you?'

'They'll want to pay you back for all the times you fought with them,' Heather said.

'Not so bold now, are you?'

At last I found my voice. 'How can you do this? I was your friend, remember? One for all and all that.'

Heather sniggered. 'You're the one who started it.'

'That's not true!'

Erin pulled her on, not wanting to listen. 'Come on, Heather. She's putting me off my tea.'

There was a sudden yell from behind us. Mrs Tasker came clattering down the corridor.

'I heard that, Erin! Heard every word. You two,' she pointed an angry finger at Erin and Heather, 'are in my office first thing in the morning!'

I saw her glance at the gates. Wizzie and the Hell Cats were standing about casually. I could almost see her putting two and two together. Me, like a wimp, hiding inside the building, scared to go out in case they were waiting for me. 'Hannah, I'll take you home.'

I knew she meant well. Mrs Tasker always means well. But she only made things worse again. She led me out into the school yard, towards the car park. In full view of everyone, she was taking me home. Like I was some terrified little girl who needed protection. And wasn't that what I was?

She drove through the school gates, and they were all standing there, watching. Wizzie, and Erin, and all the rest. Staring at me through the car window. They broke a path to let us through. I saw them snigger, make faces at me. I knew what they were thinking.

Maybe, I thought, *I should go to a new school*. Because I decided then and there, I was never coming back to this one.

CHAPTER TWENTY-NINE

All the way home, Mrs Tasker did her best to make me feel better. She is a nice woman. I could see that. She just couldn't understand what was going on.

'You just have to get over it, Hannah. I know it's hard. I can see how cruel they're being to you. But just you face up to them with your head held high, and you'll soon get through this, and find other friends.'

Other friends? I couldn't imagine it. I thanked her and she gripped my hand as I slid from the car.

'See you tomorrow, Hannah?'

But I had already decided that she wouldn't. I trudged upstairs to our flat and opened the door. The emptiness, the silence, only made me feel worse. Maybe if I'd been going home each day to a houseful of brothers and sisters my mind would have been lifted. I had too much time to think. But Mum was hardly ever here when I came home. Not her fault. She had to work. This was her late shift. She wouldn't be home for ages. Wouldn't want to face her anyway.

She'd left something for me to microwave – lasagne – but I couldn't eat anything. I even tried watching television for a while, but the film on Sky was about a teenager dying from some awful disease. Not exactly uplifting. I wanted to sleep, because at least when I was sleeping I could forget about it for a while. But when I lay on my bed, sleep just wouldn't come. My mind was too full for sleep. I went over everything again and again, and it got worse every time. What had happened already, and what was yet to come.

Finally, I got up and went into the bathroom and opened the glass cabinet over the sink.

The first thing I saw – my mum's sleeping pills.

She still kept them here, still trusted with them despite . . .

Mum's secret that everyone knew and no one spoke about.

Usually I didn't think about it either – pushed it to the very deepest corner of my mind. I thought about it now.

Remembered.

Remembered finding her on the floor when I

came in from school that day, and the note lying beside her.

Sorry, Hannah, I can't go on any more . . .

I didn't read the rest. I tore it to pieces I was so angry with her, so scared. The neighbours came and I was held back, too young to be involved. I watched them take her away on a stretcher, not knowing if she was alive or dead.

My aunt had looked after me while she was in hospital. She was angry too. She thought my mum was weak, couldn't face up to life. They hadn't spoken since.

I could never understand why she'd done it.

Dad had left, but our life wasn't that bad. She had a job. We had this nice flat. It was something inside my mother that was wrong.

And now, for the first time, I understood. When I was asleep, I could forget about what was happening. I wanted to sleep all the time.

Maybe I wanted to sleep for ever.

I stared at her box of tablets and felt my face come out in a cold sweat.

Bet they'd all be sorry then.

I pictured my mum coming home and finding me in

bed. She wouldn't worry, not then. I was always in bed early now. It would be morning before the panic would set in. She would come into my room and not be able to wake me up.

And *they* would all get the blame.

I could see the headlines.

THEY DROVE HER TO SUICIDE

And it would all come out, everything they had done to me. There would be an inquiry. An outcry. My story would be discussed on television. It would never happen again, some politician would promise.

And then, there would be my funeral.

I saw my coffin in the church, draped in white, a gold crucifix placed on top of it. And Erin, and Heather, and Rose, and all the rest would cower in the back, sobbing tears of shame. No one would talk to them. They'd be isolated. Alone.

Let them cry, I thought. A sea of tears wouldn't make up for what they'd done to me.

It would be too late.

Too late for me.

Too late for them.

All I had to do was open that bottle and swallow those tablets.

That was all.

So simple.

I would have my revenge.

CHAPTER THIRTY

How long did I stand there in the bathroom just staring at those pills? It was as if time stood still. All I could think about was how I could make them all sorry for the way they had treated me.

But I wouldn't be around to enjoy my revenge. I'd be dead and gone. I wouldn't be able to see my funeral, witness their tears of misery, see the trouble they would be in. It would only be fun if I could leap out of my coffin at the right moment and yell at them, 'Gotya!'

Erin really would pee her pants then.

And that was what brought a smile to my lips. A smile. When was the last time I had smiled? Here I was in the depths of despair, and I was smiling. It was as if the old me was fighting to get through. The old Hannah who smiled all the time, who never let anything get her down.

I tried to think straight. What was it that was lifting

my spirits from somewhere deep inside me? As if a trapped animal was struggling to get out.

The old me. A faint voice was calling to me. *Don't do it. I want to live.*

I stared at myself in the mirror. What a mess I had become. Hardly bothering to fix my hair, dark circles under my eyes, my face drawn and streaked with tears.

And why?

Because my friends had deserted me. They had turned on me. I had sworn to them that I wasn't the one who had told everyone Erin's secret, and they hadn't believed me. I had done everything to get them back. I had humiliated myself in front of the whole school, and it still wasn't enough. They wouldn't have me.

The voice inside me was getting louder, and I listened.

I had come to this because there was nowhere else for me to go. No other road for me to take. I was frightened and alone.

Yet something inside wanted them to know what they'd done to me. And pay for it.

What do you do if you're chased up a one-way street and find yourself trapped? When there's nowhere else for you to go and they're all after you?

Do you cower in a corner and plead for mercy?

No.

You turn and fight.

The voice inside me grew louder still.

It was the thought of revenge that had made me smile. But I had to be here to see that revenge, not dead and buried under the ground, food for worms.

Getting my own back on every last one of them. How great would that be?

Making them pay for what they had done to me.

I was trembling. But it wasn't fear or despair any more. It was determination. They had got me to this point. The point where I was ready to take those pills and end it all.

I suddenly realised that I would have no revenge that way. They would simply say I was weak, like my mother. I pictured those headlines again. Only this time they read.

HANNAH DRISCOLL, A VICTIM OF SUICIDE

And that would be how I would be remembered – a victim.

Not good enough, not for Hannah Driscoll.

I had let a bunch of so-called friends drag me down so low that I had no pride.

The real me had been buried under all that shame. Now she was clawing her way back. She was telling me I couldn't let them win. Her voice was bellowing in my ear now.

I could either go back to school tomorrow, cowering like a wimp, or I could stride in, with my head held high.

What was it I had always had, and they loved me for it? Attitude.

And suddenly, it was like that magical moment when a dolphin breaks the surface of the ocean and leaps into the air. I felt my attitude leap to the surface, just like that.

I felt it fill my body like blood pumping through my veins. Bringing with it new life. That's exactly how I felt. I was beginning a new life. It was the most wonderful moment I could remember.

The old me was back. She settled into my skin and filled me, and I knew nothing would make me lose her again. Mrs Tasker would kill me for all these mixed metaphors! But that was how I felt.

The old me was my real friend. No one else. And she hadn't deserted me. I had been the one who had deserted her.

I closed the door of the bathroom cabinet and

splashed my face. Then I stood up straight and stared at the new me. Did my eyes look brighter? I was sure they did. I had made my choice. I was going to school with my head held high.

Then I remembered Wizzie and her gang. They had threatened to get me. I would be easy meat. I was alone, didn't belong any more.

Wizzie and the Hell Cats were in for a shock too. They had threatened to get me?

Well, I was going to get them first.

PART 3

THE HELL CATS

CHAPTER THIRTY-ONE

My only fear was that the feeling would wear off during the night. It didn't. I woke up next morning like a tiger coming to life. To think I had even considered not waking up at all on this beautiful morning.

Even my mother noticed the difference in me. She's usually so wrapped up in herself she doesn't notice anything. I walked into the kitchen as she was filling the washing machine. 'Are you OK? Your cheeks are really flushed.'

'I feel brilliant,' I said, and that surprised her.

Her cheeks were red too. 'About yesterday, Hannah, me coming up to the school . . .' Was that only yesterday? It had seemed so important yesterday. Today, it didn't matter at all. She tried to apologise. 'Maybe I did the wrong thing coming to the school. I always do the wrong thing. But I'm a woman on my own, I haven't got anybody to support me.'

If I kept on listening to this I was afraid she'd drag me down again. So I stopped her in mid-flow. 'It's OK, Mum. Doesn't matter. Got to go.'

She dragged her hair back with her fingers. 'This early?'

'It's a nice morning for a walk,' I said.

She followed me to the door. 'Are you sure you're all right? You seem different today.'

Different wasn't the word. I was back. For weeks I had tried to sneak in the school gates, hoping no one would notice me. Today I wanted them to see me. I wanted them all to see me. It was a cold crisp morning and the sun shone on the snow-tipped purple hills. Everything looked clearer and brighter today.

Just as I arrived at the school gates, the bus pulled up beside me and Erin jumped off with Heather at her heels.

'Oh, look who's here, Heather,' she sneered. 'The wimp.'

I ignored her. I couldn't argue with that. I had been a wimp. But no more. She strode ahead of me. Why had I never noticed before what fat ankles Erin had? I had always thought she was so perfect. And Heather, always hanging on her every word as if she didn't have a mind of her own. Had I been like that too?

Erin stopped in front of me, barring my way. She swivelled round to face me. 'What time's your mum coming today . . . or is she here already? Maybe you've packed her in your rucksack.'

I didn't answer at first. I just looked at Erin. I stared and I stared. It was Erin who blinked first. 'Buzz off,' I said, and I glanced at Heather. 'And take your monkey with you.'

Heather gasped. 'Who are you calling a monkey?'

'I'll give you a mirror. You can figure it out for yourself.'

'We'll make you sorry you said that.' Erin tried to sound threatening, and do you know what? It didn't work any more. I just smiled.

'In your dreams,' I said.

I wasn't interested in them. I was just pleased they looked so baffled by my attitude. The one I was really interested in was swaggering up towards the school.

Wizzie.

Her red-streaked hair was spiked and fierce-looking and she was chewing gum. She was always chewing gum. Grace, running to catch up with her, looked even more like a horse. Chomping away at her gum too, all she needed was a nosebag and the picture would be complete. They linked arms. Grace, a head taller than Wizzie, looked as if she was holding her up.

I turned away from Erin as if she wasn't there. That must have been so annoying for her. I headed straight for Wizzie. Stopped right in front of her.

Wizzie did her 'stands back in amazement' routine, holding up her hands, mock surprise on her face. 'What have we got here, Grace?'

'She's come to beg for mercy probably,' Grace said, smug.

I didn't waste time answering that. 'You said you'd get me.' I poked Wizzie in the chest and she staggered back a few steps. 'Fine with me. But I'll pick the time and place. Today. After school. Up behind the football pitch, far away from the school so the teachers won't find out.' I paused. 'Square go.' I said that because I didn't want any knives involved, and if Wizzie agreed to a square go now, with half the school listening, she couldn't go back on it. 'You do know what a square go is, don't you, Wizzie? One at a time. Fair fight. OK?'

Then I swung past her and walked through the school gates.

*　*　*

By lunchtime news of the fight was all around the school. Moira tried her best to make me change my mind. 'You haven't a chance, Hannah. And you know what Wizzie might do . . .' Her voice trailed off. The word 'knife' unspoken.

'It's just something I've got to do, Moira,' I said.

There was a sudden bellow of laughter behind us. 'A man's gotta do what a man's gotta do!' Who else but Zak Riley? 'You think you're living in the Wild West, Driscoll. You've not gotta do anything. Get real!'

'I think she's been really brave, Zak,' Moira said.

I smiled. 'Thanks, Moira.'

'Brave? Are you kiddin', Moira? I think she's dead stupid.'

'It's better than being dead ugly,' I snapped back at him.

'And tonight, you'll just be dead.'

'Don't bet on it.'

'I've never known anybody like you in my life. You like fighting better than boys do.'

'That's because I fight better than boys do.'

Zak wasn't a fighter anyway. He was never in fights. 'Me and my mates are coming to watch you. It'll be good for a laugh.'

'I'll take you on when I finish with Wizzie.'

Zak laughed and moved off with his mates. 'I'll take along a shovel and scrape you up. You'll be like raspberry jam.'

It was then I remembered again, Wizzie's knife.

Slash! Slash!

I pictured it in my mind, gleaming in the dying sunlight as it hacked and slashed in front of my face.

It was the only thing that freaked me out. Wizzie's knife. The rumour was she always had it on her, the scars on her neck and arms evidence of the knife fights she had been in. How bold I had been when I'd had my friends about me. Wizzie's knife hadn't bothered me then. But now I was alone, and I thought about the old woman again. She'd been threatened with a knife. So why should Wizzie draw the line at using it on me? Yet the more I thought about it, the more I realised that she wouldn't risk her reputation by using a knife when I had none.

Square go, we had said, and that's what it would be: a square go. There were certain rules we all stuck to and that was one of them. If there was going to be a lot of people watching, even more reason for her to fight fair.

The thought of an audience kind of bothered me.

Maybe I shouldn't have challenged them so publicly. But it was too late now. From now on I would have no regrets about anything. So the whole school were going to be there to watch? Good. They would all be waiting for me to be humiliated. I was determined to put up a good show. I wouldn't win, I knew that. But no one would ever call me a wimp again.

CHAPTER THIRTY-TWO

They were all there, Grace and Lauren and Sonya, and in the middle of them, Wizzie. I'd take her first, I decided, remembering from somewhere that if you cut off the head, the body couldn't survive. I think I'd heard it in a zombie film, but then, what else were the Hell Cats but a gang of zombies?

Wizzie turned and stared at me as I approached. 'Oh, here comes Rocky!' And then with a wild tribal roar that was meant to take me by surprise I suppose, she threw herself at me.

But I wasn't surprised. I had been prepared for anything, even this. I side-stepped her and she landed with a thud on the ground. There was a cheer from the crowd. Wizzie was on her feet in an instant, her eyes blazing. She lunged at me and I grabbed her hair. It was a great target with those spikes of hers. I pulled her head back and kicked the back of her legs. She was down again, this time on her back. I was on top of her in a second, straddling her chest, pinning her wrists to the ground. 'Give up!' I said.

'Never,' she said through gritted teeth. I thought I had her, but with a sudden burst of strength, she arched her back and threw me off her. I tumbled to the ground and only a quick roll to the side stopped her landing on me. Her fist caught the side of my face, and sent my head spinning. I got to my feet quickly and launched myself at her. I wasn't going to give her a minute.

This time we both tumbled together on the ground. She had me by the hair. I almost wished I'd had the nerve to tug at the earring on her eyebrow, but I couldn't bring myself to do that. Instead I punched her on the side of the head so hard her eyes went squinty. She pushed me off her and we both got to our feet. But my punch had knocked Wizzie for six. She was having trouble focussing and took a step back, to let someone else take her place.

That someone was Grace. 'My turn,' she said and she squared up to me, stepping in front of Wizzie.

The sweat was pouring off me, but I still wasn't scared. I was too keyed up to be scared. Grace Morgan was big. As she lumbered towards me I realised just how big. But she wasn't fast. I lowered my head and charged at her and sent her reeling to the ground. There was another roar from the crowd. A different kind of roar this time. All of a sudden they were on my side. I could tell. They wanted me to win.

'Behind you, Hannah!' Someone yelled it from the crowd. I turned just in time to stop Lauren leaping on my back. I grabbed at her, spun her round and sent her tumbling on top of Grace.

Sonya was waiting for me next. She let out a scream and ran at me. Sonya's a big girl too. And fat with it. She hit me so hard we both fell back.

I was on the ground and almost waiting for the rest of Wizzie's gang to jump on me, but they didn't. That wouldn't have been a square go and they knew it. Instead it was Sonya who leapt at me again, but I held up my hands and pushed her back.

I was like a wild animal. I was on top of her. She grabbed my ears and rolled me over. I butted her in the face, and that hurt me as much as it hurt her. But at least my nose didn't bleed. Hers did. I could see anger in her eyes as she tasted her own blood. 'I'll kill you for that!'

'Try it.'

And she almost did. Anger gave her more strength. She was up and leapt at me again. This time I couldn't dodge her or keep my balance. I began to topple with Sonya on top of me. Her blood dripped on my hair, into my face. She was ready to butt me back as she had me pinned to the ground. I was done for.

What had Wizzie done to get free of me? I did the same to Sonya, arching my back, lifting my whole body to send Sonya tumbling off me. I was on her in an instant.

The crowd were going mad, cheering and clapping. I sat astride Sonya, pinning her arms to the ground with my knees, the way I had with Wizzie. Where were the rest of the Hell Cats? I waited for them to jump in, especially Wizzie. But they didn't. They stood together, watching me, and I couldn't tell what they were thinking. I looked from them to the mad cheering crowd. I could see Erin and the rest, ashen-faced. They were standing well at the back. But my eyes only flicked past them.

I looked round at everyone else, relishing the moment. Watching their faces – amazed, and pleased for me too.

I lifted my hand in the air, thumbs up, then I turned

it slowly so my thumb was down, just as if we were in a Roman arena and I was a gladiator.

It was to be the crowd's decision what happened next, and they knew it.

There was a lull in the cheering, then with a roar that almost split my eardrums, almost every hand was held in the air, thumbs up.

And then they went wild.

Sonya began to struggle again. 'Thank God for that!' she shouted. 'Now get off me!'

I leapt to my feet and turned to look round at everyone again. Then I took a slow bow to the cheers and the applause.

It was a wonderful moment.

I knew I had won more than a fight that day.

CHAPTER THIRTY-THREE

I got home before Mum and had my bloodstained clothes (their blood not mine, I'm glad to say) in the washing machine and dried even before she came in. I was in my pyjamas sitting in front of the TV when she first noticed my face. My eye was swollen and my cheek was covered in scratches.

'What happened to you?' She said it in a what's-she-going-to-tell-me-now? kind of tone.

'I fell in PE. Right off the wall bars.' The lie came easily and I could see the relief in her face. She didn't even question it.

'Did you have a good day? Did you have any more trouble?'

'No trouble at all. In fact, I had a brilliant day.'

She looked as if a weight had been lifted from her shoulders. You hear that expression all the time, but you don't think what it really means. But I watched my mum stand straighter. Her face brightened, and I suppose for the first time I realised just how worried she must have been about me.

'You see, sometimes your mother can do something right. That's because I went up to the school. That's what's made them stop.'

And perhaps she was right. Mum going up to the school had been the thing that changed everything.

The last straw for me.

'I think that is what made the difference, Mum,' I told her. And she beamed at me.

'Really?' She looked so happy, I felt like crying. 'I'm so glad about that.'

Mum and I had a lovely night together. She made shortbread, and she makes the best shortbread in the world, though she never believes it. We watched a horror film on video. I just knew everything was going to be different now, because I was going to make it different. Even with my mum. I understood now how you can get to such a point of despair you just want to end it, to sleep for ever. When it had happened to Mum a doctor had told me it was a cry for help. I didn't understand what he meant then, but I did now. She had cried for help, and no one, certainly not me, had reached out to help her.

* * *

Next day, when I walked into school, every eye was on me. And there was something in their gaze that hadn't been there for a long time.

Respect.

Nobody likes a wimp. And I had been a wimp for too long.

It still made me angry, thinking about how I had let my so-called friends treat me. How I'd behaved too. Never again. I would have my revenge somehow.

Zak and his mates were all gathered together in the corridor. He couldn't resist a quip. 'Hey, Driscoll, good to see the old Hannah back. Where have you been hiding her?'

Had it been so plain to see that even Zak Riley had noticed it?

'She's been on holiday. But she's back, for good,' I snapped back, and I swept past him.

Mrs Tasker stormed into class, and she was livid. Her eyes settled on me. 'There have been reports of a fight near this school yesterday. I believe some of our pupils were involved, and to make matters worse, those pupils were girls.'

This set the whole class laughing. Zak shouted up to her, 'Mrs Tasker, it's not lassies we've got in this school, it's the devil's daughters.'

Mrs Tasker went spare. 'This is no laughing matter!' she yelled and we all shut up. 'Hannah. What happened to your face?'

'Walked into a door, Mrs Tasker,' I said at once.

She looked even madder. Her eyes moved to Wizzie. Today Wizzie's nose was like a beetroot stuck on her face, same colour too. 'And what happened to you?'

'I walked into the same door. We should be suing for compensation. That's a really dangerous door.'

The class erupted in laughter again, and it took Mrs Tasker ages to get any order back. Meanwhile, Wizzie turned to look at me, and for the first time there wasn't any malice in her gaze, just curiosity. She waited for me as we left class. 'Want to meet up wi' us later?'

'For another fight? How many times do you want me to beat you?'

'We let you win. Felt sorry for you.'

'In your dreams, McLeod. Anyway, what do you want to talk to me about?'

Grace butted in. 'I'm just telling you now, Driscoll, this isn't my idea.'

'Shut up, Grace,' Wizzie turned back to me. 'Meet us at the bus shelters after school.'

I didn't want to. Didn't want anything more to do with the Hell Cats. But I was curious. What could they possibly want to talk to me about? Giving them boxing lessons?

Mrs Tasker wanted to talk to me too. She came running down the corridor after me and pulled me back. Yesterday I would have been mortified if she'd done that. Everyone seeing her singling me out? Not today. Today I stood tall. 'Are you going to tell me what happened, Hannah? I know you were involved in that fight. Did that lot jump you, or what?'

'I told you, Mrs Tasker, it was an accident.' I stared straight into her face as if it was all the truth.

'How can I help you if you don't confide in me?'

But I didn't need her help now. It was too late. 'Honest, I'm fine.'

She shook her head in disgust. 'Are you frightened to grass on them? They'll never know you told me. I won't let them know.'

That almost made me smile. Here I was in the corridor with her, with all eyes on us. They'd never know . . . ? I don't think.

'Everything's sorted now,' I said.

Now she really did look mad. 'If that's your attitude I don't see how you can expect any help.' And she stormed away from me.

Too little, too late, I thought and then I forgot about her. I forgot about everything except what Wizzie wanted to talk to me about after school.

They were all there waiting for me at the bus stop. Was I afraid? No. They didn't look threatening. Wizzie was lounging against the wall. Lauren was sitting on her rucksack. Grace and Sonya were muttering together, about me, I was sure. They didn't want to have this talk with me at all.

I stopped dead in front of them. No fear. 'OK, what's this about?'

'I d-d-don't like you,' Sonya said.

'Feeling's mutual,' I said.

'I don't like you either,' Grace said, sticking up for her friend.

'Just because I kicked your butt?' I pretended to study it. 'Mind you, it would be hard to miss. It's a big target.'

Wizzie actually laughed. Even Lauren managed a smile. But Grace swayed on her feet, and if Wizzie hadn't been there I was sure she would have flown at me.

'See you, Driscoll – you've got style.' I was totally gobsmacked when Wizzie said that. 'That took a lot of guts to take us on yesterday.'

Grace tutted and Wizzie turned on her. 'Be honest, Grace. That did take a lot of guts.'

But Grace wasn't about to give in. 'I'd like to have seen them spread out over the road,' she said.

'Don't listen to Grace. She's really a softie at heart. Anyway,' Wizzie went on, 'me and the lassies have been talking, and we've got a proposition for you.' She paused, watched for my reaction to her next words. 'How would you like to become a Hell Cat?'

CHAPTER THIRTY-FOUR

For a moment I thought I'd heard her wrong. Or maybe I was dreaming. Had Wizzie really asked me to join her gang? I was so taken aback I didn't know what to say. Just stood there, staring.

Wizzie started waving her hands about in front of my face. 'Hello! Is anybody in?' She looked at Lauren. 'The lights are on but nobody's home.'

It seemed ages before I found my voice. 'You're asking me to join your gang?'

'Count me out of this!' Grace snapped the words out, too close to my face. 'I think it's the worst idea they've ever had.'

'They'? So it wasn't just Wizzie's idea.

'I'm wi' Grace on this.' Sonya moved a step closer to Grace.

'See, Grace and Sonya are against it. And me and Lauren are for it. And because this is a democracy . . . majority wins.'

'It was an equal vote,' I reminded her. 'Two against two.'

Wizzie just shrugged. 'Aye, but I arm-wrestled them for the other vote. And I'm bigger than they are.' She wasn't actually. She was the smallest of the lot, tiny in size and build, but there was something about Wizzie that made her seem bigger. 'So . . . what's your answer?'

'What's the catch?' There had to be a catch. I was sure of it.

'You're a good fighter,' Lauren said.

'I don't want to spend all my time fighting.'

'Neither do we.' Grace still sounded as if she'd like to grab me by the hair and drag me along the street. 'We always have a great laugh, the whole lot of us. Brilliant mates we are. Not like your nancy pals. Ooo, the Lip Gloss Girls.' She pretended to put lipstick on her big horsey lips.

But we'd had brilliant times too . . . 'They're not my pals,' I reminded them.

'Well, there ye are. You've not got any mates. We could be your mates.' Wizzie said it as if it was an offer I'd be mad to refuse.

'What would I want you lot for my mates for?'

'Desperation?' Lauren suggested.

I turned on her. 'I'd have to be desperate to join your gang.'

'What did I tell you?' Grace turned on Wizzie angrily. 'What do we want her for?'

'Give me one good reason why I should join the Hell Cats.'

Wizzie grinned. 'I'll give you a great one. Because you want to watch that Erin's face when she sees you walking into that canteen wi' us.'

And at that moment, they had me. I knew then I wouldn't say no. I shrugged casually and told them I'd let them know my decision next day at school – but that decision was already made.

I was going to join the Hell Cats.

CHAPTER THIRTY-FIVE

In my dreams that night I pictured Erin's face when she first saw me with them. What a moment that would be. I woke up and still knew it was the right thing to do. The right thing because it would annoy Erin so much. But it had to be done in the right way.

It had to be the perfect moment for her to find out. I went through all the possibilities in my mind. I imagined myself standing with the Hell Cats at the school gates, pictured Erin stepping off her bus and practically falling over us – saw the look on her face, shock, horror . . .

But no, just not dramatic enough.

Then I pictured the scene in class when I would suddenly turn to Wizzie and say nonchalantly, 'So, where are we going tonight?'

No, she could miss that completely. Erin might be polishing her claws at that point.

At last I figured out the best time for them to find out. Just as good old Wizzie had said. In the canteen, so that the whole school could witness the great moment.

I could hardly wait for lunchtime next day. I was deliberately late for school because I didn't want to see anyone outside the gates. I didn't even glance at any of them in class. I blanked everyone, waiting for my moment. If watching films had taught me anything, it was how to make an entrance.

I was almost the last pupil into the canteen. I collected my tray and waited in the queue for food. I didn't look at anyone, didn't talk to anyone either. Then I began the long walk to a table. I could feel everyone's eyes on me. For so long I'd felt such a fool trying to find a table that would actually have me. Usually I tripped and could hear all the murmured giggles. I didn't feel a fool today. I walked straight-backed and full of confidence right past Erin and the rest at our table.

No. Not our table. Not now. It would never be our table again.

They pretended not to look, but I knew as soon as I walked on by their gazes would follow me, wondering where I was going to sit.

The Hell Cats had a table too. They never ate off it.

They sat on top of it, or lay along it, or rested their feet on it. Today Wizzie was lying across the table on her belly, leaning her face on her hands, watching me heading towards them. She was always in trouble for it, but she didn't care. Grace and Sonya were sitting on either side of her, throwing cake at each other. Lauren wasn't even looking my way. She was sitting on the table too, eating an apple.

And I stopped right beside them.

I could feel everyone in the canteen hold their breath, expecting trouble. Wondering what was going to happen next.

I could almost hear the communal gasp at what did happen.

'You're only allowed to sit here if you're one of us,' Wizzie said.

I looked at Grace. 'Move your lardass, Grace, I'm sitting.' And I plonked myself down beside her.

Grace moved up. Wizzie slid on to the seat beside her. Lauren looked up and smiled. They moved up. They welcomed me in.

And I sat down.

It was a great moment. There, in front of the whole school, they were letting everyone know I belonged,

194

and I was letting everyone see where my loyalties would lie from now on.

Why did I always think like the movies? During that long walk, it was as if the sound had been turned down, I couldn't hear anything. As soon as I sat down the noise of the canteen at lunchtime was switched up to full blast.

'See if you say one more thing about the size of my bum I'll thump ye,' Grace said.

I pretended to be shocked. 'Are you allowed to thump your mates in this gang?'

'No way.' Lauren offered me a bit of chewing gum. 'But you're not allowed to slag them off either.'

'We stick up for our m-m-mates,' Sonya stuttered deliberately, daring me to say a word about it. I didn't. I never would again.

I looked at Grace. 'OK,' I said. 'Sorry.'

Grace looked away from me and I knew it would take more than an apology to make Grace happy about me being her mate.

I could see a lot of puzzled stares as I sat there. Everyone wondering what was going on. It made me smile. A mystery, and I love mysteries.

Suddenly Heather came hurrying up to us, her tray

in her hands. Her mouth was hanging open and she couldn't take her eyes off me. 'What are you doing sitting here . . . with *them*?' She looked around as if they were a bad smell. 'Have they kidnapped you?'

'Do you care? Will you pay the ransom?' I asked.

'I'd tell them to keep you.'

Wizzie blew a pink bubble. 'Might just do that,' she said.

Heather didn't know what to say next. 'Let me by,' she finally muttered, staring at Grace's big feet spread out in the passage.

I spread my feet out too. 'Go another way,' I told her.

She stood for a moment, unsure of what to do, shaking with anger. Then she turned on her heel and stamped away from us.

'Heather won't stand up to anyone on her own,' I said.

Wizzie raised the eyebrow with the earring in it. It jiggled. 'That's good to know,' she said.

'So, is that me in?' I asked.

'Not quite,' Lauren said.

'Think it's going to be that easy?' Grace said.

'We've decided you've got to do something to prove you're worthy to be one of us.' Lauren told me.

'You mean, kicking your butts all over the football pitch wasn't enough?'

'We let you win,' Grace said and turned her back on me.

'Is this, like, a test?' I asked. I didn't like the sound of this. I'd heard about some of the boy gangs in the town and the daft initiation tests they had to get into the gang. One boy had supposedly died in very mysterious circumstances during one of those tests.

No. I wasn't doing anything that involved grievous bodily harm, especially if it was my body that was going to be harmed. I wasn't going to tie myself down on the railway tracks either, and try to escape before the next train splattered me all over the place. I wasn't that desperate to be a Hell Cat.

'So what is it I have to do?' I asked.

'Nothing much,' Wizzie said. 'Just impress us.'

CHAPTER THIRTY-SIX

Impress them? How was I ever going to impress the Hell Cats with their wild ways? They had done everything.

Abseil off the Erskine Bridge? Kidnap the prime minister?

But I knew I had to think of something. And it had to be good.

I hardly saw where I was going as I walked home. I was so lost in thought I almost fell over Junior Bonnar, and his three cases, coming out of our close.

'I've just been at your door, Terry,' he said.

'Have you? What for?'

'This is me off to Majorca.' (He pronounced it Matchorca.) 'Me and my bird,' he went on. 'I asked your mammy if I could leave my keys with her, and she said yes, the darlin'. So I put them through your letterbox.'

A taxi drew up then and Junior waved it down. 'That's my taxi now,' he said.

I stood by as he climbed into the back. 'If your mammy could water my plants I'd be really grateful, hen.'

'No problem, Junior.' He looked so excited to be going on holiday, like a little boy. 'Have a nice time!' I called after him.

He stuck his head out of the car window. 'Thanks, Terry,' he said, grinning. 'By the way, my car keys are there as well, so you can use the car any time you want. OK?'

I stood waving Junior off, beaming like an idiot. 'You can use the car any time you want,' he had said.

It was like a gift falling into my hands. Junior's car. I knew then what I was going to do to impress the Hell Cats. I was going to take them for a joyride.

The car keys lay on the mat behind the door, along with one of Junior's badly spelt notes.

I picked up the keys and sat for ages, just staring at them.

Junior was off with his 'bird'. (Junior had a 'bird'? He was full of surprises.) He'd be already at the airport enjoying the duty-free. This was Mum's night for her Spanish class. She went straight to the local college after work. She wouldn't be home until late. Mum need never know. I would be back before she would . . . either that or my body parts would be scattered all over a dark and lonely road somewhere.

Junior had let me drive his car round the car park so often, sitting beside me, showing me how to use the accelerator, the brake and clutch. Surely going out on the road couldn't be that different?

But what if Wizzie and the rest didn't think it was so daring? They probably went joyriding every night for a laugh. Well, I decided, I would have to take that chance.

I phoned Wizzie first. 'You contact the others. I'll meet you at the retail park.'

'The retail park?' Wizzie sounded surprised.

The only retail park we had in the town was full of empty, vacant shops.

'That'll be deserted this time of night,' she went on. 'Hey, you're not planning to turn into a vampire, are you? That kind of shock we don't need.'

'Wait and see,' I said mysteriously.

Of course the retail park would be deserted. That's why it was perfect. Lots of wide turning areas, lots of space. Nobody about. After all, I didn't actually want to trash Junior's car.

I felt like Alice in Wonderland as soon as I slipped into the front seat. As if I'd shrunk in size. The car seemed too big. As it was I could hardly see over the steering wheel. I must be mad. What was I thinking about?

Then my nerve came back. Junior was one sandwich short of a picnic. If Junior could drive, then so could I. Go for it, girl!

I made so much noise revving up the engine I was sure the neighbours would come shooting out of their houses. Even when I pushed my foot down on the accelerator the car didn't budge. Until I remembered I hadn't let the handbrake off. When it finally did move, it chugged and bumped across the car park. A couple of women coming out of one of the flats glanced my way. But they were used to Junior's car doing wheelies in the car park. They looked away almost at once.

So far, so good. I was moving. Now all I had to do was make it to the retail park.

I took the lonely back road to avoid traffic lights and junctions. Something told me I was meant to change gear at some point, but since my lessons with Junior had never got that far, I didn't bother. I made it there anyway. I chugged into the retail park and saw the Hell Cats gathered together under a street light. They turned and stared when they heard the car. They were like rabbits caught in the headlights as they watched it heading straight for them.

I saw their surprise turn to alarm as I careered towards them. I was going faster. How was I supposed to stop this thing? My mind was a total blank.

'Get out of the way!' I waved my arms about frantically. They didn't need to be told twice. They separated and ran off in different directions. I was heading for a brick wall. If I didn't do something quick, it would be concertina time for me and the car. Finally, I got my head together, slammed on the brakes and pulled at the handbrake at the same time. With a screech and a roar, I came to a halt.

They all came running after me.

I rolled down the window and grinned. 'I think that was an emergency stop!'

Wizzie threw back her head and laughed. And I knew I had done it, because suddenly, they were all laughing. Even Grace.

'I didn't think there was anybody behind the wheel! I

couldn't see you. The invisible driver.' Wizzie laughed.

'Where did you get the car?' Lauren asked.

'A friend,' I said casually.

'This is brilliant,' Sonya said, and she didn't even stutter.

I was so pleased they were pleased I accidentally let the handbrake off and almost rolled into a brick wall again. 'Get in quick!' I shouted. 'I can't stop this thing properly.'

Grace hauled open the back door. 'Can you drive?'

'Well, I can't stop it, I can't steer it and I can't change gears. But otherwise, Michael Schumacher eat your heart out.'

Lauren clambered in the back beside Grace. 'Where are we goin'?'

'Pick a place. As long as it doesn't have any turns in the road, we might survive.'

Sonya squeezed in beside Grace and Lauren. 'No, honestly, whose c-car is it?'

'Professional secret,' I said.

Wizzie threw herself into the front seat beside me. 'You stole a car! Bold bitch!'

I didn't tell her any different. I liked how she said that – 'bold bitch'.

'Let's go for a spin,' I said.

Getting the car into reverse was my first problem. It didn't help that they were all shouting advice at me.

'It's something to do with that stick thing.'

'I think you have to press one of those buttons.'

'Have we got to get out and push this blinkin' thing?'

In the end that was exactly what they had to do. The four of them leaning on the bonnet and turning me round. But once we were out of that car park, I was on a roll. The retail park was on the edge of town and the street it was on led to a lonely coast road.

'Aren't you supposed to have the lights on?' Lauren suggested, and for the first time I realised that I had been driving along the road in a dark car.

I switched on the radio, the windscreen wipers and the hazard lights before I finally remembered where the right switch was, and the road ahead blazed with light.

'Ah, this is so much better. I can see where I'm going now.'

Lauren let out a sudden screech. 'Ah! What's that?' She pointed to something squashed flat on the road ahead of us.

'Looks like a hedgehog,' Wizzie said, peering closer.

'Is it dead?' Lauren was almost out the window, looking at it.

'Well, it's certainly not sunbathing, Lauren,' I told her, and suddenly, we were all laughing.

I couldn't remember when I had laughed so much. We screamed as we wheelspinned round corners, we made up stories on the dark roads to frighten ourselves, and turned up Junior's CD to full blast, singing at the top of our voices.

I think at some point I even managed to get the car into second gear.

It seemed ages later when I dropped them all off at the retail park again. But it was less than an hour. We were still laughing.

'We really should do this more often,' Wizzie said. 'Who says we'll steal a bus the next time?'

They all stood waving at me as I drove off, and it was only as I parked Junior's car (perhaps a little too close to the BMW beside it) that it occurred to me that, by the time I'd left them, I'd felt as if we'd been friends for ever. They were my mates.

I think we'd bonded.

CHAPTER THIRTY-SEVEN

I swaggered into school next day and was folded into the group of them as they stood in the corridor. 'Crashed any good cars lately?' Lauren asked.

'I nearly did. Twice after I left you. And then I forgot to put the handbrake on. The car rolled away and I think it might have put a dent in Mrs Miller's BMW.' It was an exaggeration, a little lie, but I didn't care. Then I shrugged. 'But everybody knows Junior's a rotten driver. He'll get the blame. He'll probably think it was him as well. He's got a memory like a sieve.'

'Is that Junior Bonnar you're talking about? Was it his car?' Wizzie asked.

'Yeah, do you know him?'

'He went to school with my brother.'

'Was that the young offenders' institute?' Lauren laughed.

'No, it was not.' Wizzie sounded annoyed and Lauren

immediately changed the subject. But I knew what school she was talking about. Junior had only ever gone to one school. A special needs school in the town. I could see Wizzie was sorry she'd mentioned it, so I said nothing.

Then we walked the yard, arm in arm, and it was exciting to see the looks on everyone's faces. Hannah Driscoll, now best mates with her arch enemies, all in just a few days.

Erin just couldn't handle it. She confronted me in the changing rooms for PE. Her face was like thunder.

'Slumming it a bit, aren't you?'

'Actually, I think I'm moving up in the world,' I snapped right back to her. I wasn't angry, or apologetic. I was funny, the way I used to be. Why couldn't I have been like this last week, during all those weeks when they had made my life such a misery?

I could see Erin didn't like the change in me. Good. She tossed her strawberry blonde hair and pouted her lips. Once I would have thought she looked cool. Now, she just looked stupid.

Just then Heather and Rose came into the changing rooms, looking for Erin. They surrounded me. 'Oh, look who it is – the girl who's found new levels to sink to.'

They were trying to humiliate me, the three of them, standing round me, blocking me in. Trying to make me afraid. Just a week ago they would have managed it. Now they just made me laugh. They looked so stupid, standing there trying to act tough. They suddenly looked to me like silly little girls playing games. Was that the way we had always looked to Wizzie and the rest? Now that I was seeing them from the other point of view, they weren't scary at all. They were a joke.

Heather shoved me, expecting me to shove back, or maybe to be scared. I didn't even stumble. I only laughed. That shook her. 'What's so funny?' she said.

'You. You're just so pathetic, Heather.'

Rose punched my arm. 'What's happened to you?'

Erin pulled her away. 'Don't even ask her. Leave her be, Rose. She's not worth bothering about.'

'Scared, are you?' I asked, and Erin turned on me. There was red-hot anger in her eyes.

'At least we wouldn't have fought you all at once, like your new mates did.'

'I took them one at a time, square go, and I've discovered you can trust them to give you a square go.'

'You could trust us.'

'Could I? You proved the kind of friends you are.' I

stood up to them. I wasn't afraid.

I saw what was in all their eyes then. It was Rose's question they wanted answered. In just a few days, what had happened to me?

I don't know what would have happened next if Mrs Carter, the PE teacher, hadn't bounced into the changing rooms. She took one look at us and bellowed, 'What's going on here? Are you all right, Hannah?' She looked at me the way I had seen her looking at me so often lately. As if I was the poor little victim, the one she had to protect.

I got to my feet and pushed Heather aside. 'I'm perfectly fine, Mrs Carter. The girls here were just asking me advice on how to get rid of bad breath. But personally, I think they're past any help.'

I could almost feel the daggers zooming from their eyes. I ignored them. I was enjoying myself. Why had I let them bring me down so low? They were nothing. And what had changed me? Not just becoming one of the Hell Cats. No. Not even fighting Wizzie and winning. No. I knew what had happened to me.

It was the fact that I had vowed never to be anybody's victim again.

CHAPTER THIRTY-EIGHT

That night was one of Mum's early shifts. She had settled herself in front of the television to watch her favourite detective serial as I was getting ready to go out. 'Where are you going?'

'Just going to meet my mates, Mum.'

She looked up at me and smiled. 'I've waited so long to hear you say that. I knew it was only a matter of time before you all got together again. Girls fall in and out all the time. It never lasts.'

She thought it was her lovely Erin and friends I was meeting up with. She'd go spare if she knew who it really was. So I didn't tell her.

She came with me to the door. 'Now remember, don't be late. Have you got your mobile with you? Well, you go and have a good time.'

I left her happy. She'd enjoy her programme all the more now. Why should I spoil it? She'd find out who my mates were soon enough.

I met them in the town centre. We all turned up, and then walked like Amazons, arm in arm, through the mall. We broke up for no one. Anyone who wanted past had to walk round us. It was brilliant!

One group of girls looked as if they weren't going to move. They saw us coming, linked arms and locked themselves together.

'Tilda and her mates,' Wizzie whispered. 'From up my estate.' She said it as if it belonged to her. 'Mingers.'

I would have laughed if I hadn't felt so tense. Mingers – what we had called Wizzie and the Hell Cats – was what she was calling another gang she considered lower than her.

The Mingers looked as if they were spoiling for trouble.

My first fight alongside the Hell Cats. I didn't want to let them down. Yet I was scared. What kind of a fight would this be? They came from Wizzie's estate, the hardest in town. Dirty fighters? Would Wizzie produce that famous knife of hers? Would they have knives too?

Wizzie swaggered up ahead of us, pushed herself right against them. 'Sorry, I never saw you there. You've lost that much weight, Tilda. Have you been on a diet?'

It was the last thing I expected her to say. Lauren squeezed my arm to keep me quiet.

Tilda narrowed her eyes. 'You winding me up, Wizzie?'

Tilda looked as if she ate a diet of chips, chocolate and cream cakes. I was trying to keep my face straight. Lauren joined in. 'Right enough, Tilda. I can see it myself. You've definitely lost weight.'

Tilda tried not to smirk. She turned to her mates. 'I told you that doughnut diet was workin'. C'mon, lassies.' They all followed her, glaring at us as they went.

'I thought we were in for a fight there,' I whispered.

'Wi' Tilda?' Wizzie said. 'Not worth the effort. We could beat them easy.'

Wizzie waited till we'd turned a corner, out of sight of Tilda and her mates, before she bent over and roared with laughter. 'That Tilda is thick as a brick. Lost weight! She looks as if she swallowed a balloon.'

We were all laughing then, except for Grace. 'I did really think she looked thinner,' she said, and that only made us laugh all the more.

So we walked and laughed, me mostly with relief.

And I felt good.

And that was the first night I met the Black Widows.

I saw them striding it out through the centre as if they owned the place. Older than us, they were all dressed in black. Even their lips were painted black.

Wizzie began to wave wildly at them. 'My mates from up the estate,' she said.

One of them waved back and Wizzie swaggered over to talk to them.

'Who on earth is that?' I turned to ask Lauren. Her face was grim. 'They look as if somebody dug them up from the grave.'

'They call themselves the B-Black Widows,' Sonya said.

I almost laughed at that. The Black Widows indeed! Lauren saw my smile. She shook her head. 'They're nothing to laugh at, Hannah. They're really bad. I wish Wizzie would keep away from them.'

'They live on Wizzie's street. It's hard for her to keep away from them,' Grace said, watching Wizzie closely.

I looked over at Wizzie too. She was laughing with these other girls, as if she was one of them, their mate. As if she was trying to impress them.

A moment later, she came walking back to us. 'They

are such a laugh. Bold as brass.'

Lauren wasn't smiling. 'You don't want to have anything to do wi' them, Wizzie. They're a bad lot.'

'No, they're alright. Honest.' She dared us to argue with her. None of us did.

Except me, of course. I couldn't keep my mouth shut. 'Is that them away back to the graveyard?'

Wizzie looked at me, ready for an argument. I grinned. Suddenly, she slapped me on the back and grinned too. 'Very funny.'

CHAPTER THIRTY-NINE

'I wish I had the money to go to the pictures,' Grace complained as we passed the cinema. 'But I'm skint till Friday.'

'I can give you a loan of money, Grace,' Sonya said.

'Should tell you,' Wizzie said to me, 'if you want anything, ask Sonya – generous to a fault. Always the first to offer.' She blew a bubble. 'Don't ask me. I'm tight.'

'Not tight, Wizzie.' Lauren squeezed her arm. 'Just usually skint.'

'That was a nice thing to say, Wizzie, thanks,' Sonya said without a stutter. I'd noticed Sonya hardly ever stuttered when she was alone with us. I was sure half the time she did it deliberately to wind everyone up.

But Lauren had told me different. 'It's only when she talks to other people, she gets nervous.'

'Nothing on at the pictures anyway, Grace,' Wizzie

complained. She pointed at the posters. 'Only some daft girlie picture.'

I was glad I'd kept my mouth shut. I had been just about to say I wanted to see that daft girlie picture. It was the kind of film the Lip Gloss Girls always made a point of going to see. 'Girl Power!' Erin would yell as we marched into the cinema.

Now I saw how stupid we must have looked. Girl Power indeed. No wonder they called us the Lip Gloss Girls. The Hell Cats didn't need to go to girlie films. There was nothing girlie about them.

Out of uniform, Lauren dressed in the weirdest outfits. Tonight she was wearing a battered leather jacket passed down from her sister, and bright yellow cropped trousers. Her hair looked as if she'd slept in it, and she had it tied up with assorted baubles of all colours. 'I like to look funky,' she said.

'Have you done your homework for old Malcolm?' Sonya asked me as we walked on.

'I hope you didn't ask me to join so I could help with your homework. I'm rubbish at maths.'

'Tell him you couldn't finish it. Make up some sob story. Your cat died and you're in mourning, or something.' Wizzie laughed. 'I'm going to tell him my

Rottweiler ate my jotter.'

'Sounds like the title of a book,' I said. '*A Rottweiler Ate My Jotter.*'

Grace looked at her. 'You don't have a Rottweiler, Wizzie.'

'Everybody else on our street does. I could borrow one of theirs.' Wizzie gave her a shove. 'Grace, it was a joke! Right.'

Grace still looked as if she didn't understand what the joke was.

I began to laugh and couldn't stop.

'It wasn't that funny,' Wizzie said.

'It's just . . . I didn't think I would be running about with the Hell Cats and talking about maths homework. That's what we used to talk about as well.'

Grace cut in. 'Don't dare say we have anything in common with that lot.'

Lauren agreed. 'No, we'd never turn on a mate like them. We stick up for each other.'

'But be fair,' I said. 'Erin thought I'd told everybody she wet the bed. That must have been mega embarrassing for her.'

'And did you tell on her?' Lauren asked me.

'No. I would never grass up a mate. It was a secret,

and I know how to keep a secret.'

'Everybody's got secrets,' Wizzie said. 'Hers was nothing special. So how did she not believe you?'

'I suppose she thought as I was the only one she had ever told, who else could it be?' Here I was, practically sticking up for Erin. Would I never learn? 'But it wasn't me,' I went on. 'Somebody must have been listening.' My face went red as I suddenly remembered who I suspected *had* been listening. Lauren's sister.

Lauren didn't get mad. Instead she burst out laughing. 'And you thought it was our Ellen. Even if she could hear you, she wouldn't care. She's rubbish at passing on gossip.'

'Next to Sonya,' Wizzie said, 'her sister, Ellen, is the nicest lassie you'll ever meet. She makes Mother Teresa look like Adolf Hitler.'

I glanced at Sonya. She was blushing with pleasure at the compliment.

So it definitely hadn't been Lauren's sister. The mystery was still there. Who was it who had spread the story?

'Anyway, it was a whole load of rubbish for nothing,' Wizzie went on. 'So, she pees the bed. Who cares?'

'Five-minute wonder,' Grace agreed.

'You don't think it's the most embarrassing thing in the world?'

Wizzie looked at me as if I was daft. 'You've got to be kidding.'

'But that Erin's really clever, you have to admit it,' Lauren said.

'How do you mean, clever?' I asked.

Wizzie answered me, as if they had discussed this before. 'One minute everybody's talking about Erin's "little problem".' She sketched the inverted commas in with her fingers. 'And the next she's managed to turn all the attention on to you. Everybody forgot Erin. Who mentions Erin's little problem now? That was fly. She's manipulative.'

Lauren choked on her chewing gum. 'She's what?! Have you just swallowed a dictionary? Manipul . . . wha'?'

'Heard it on the telly last night. It was a film about this lassie, she's a serial killer, who makes everybody do what she wants . . . only they don't realise it. They think she's really their friend. And I thought it sounded like Erin Brodie.'

I had never thought about it like that, but it was true. Erin was manipulative. She told me I was her best friend. Had she told Heather that too, and Rose? Winding us all around her fingers. And I had fallen for it. How could I have been such an idiot?

'I'm going to get her back for that,' I said.

Wizzie grinned. 'Good,' she said. 'We'll help you.'

And our loud tribal roar echoed through the mall.

CHAPTER FORTY

And so I became one of the Hell Cats. We spent the days at school lolling on the stairs, not letting anyone past, and at night, usually we would meet up and strut our stuff through the town centre. I began to dress like them, wearing my school skirt too short, my blouse open at the neck and my tie always loose. A disgrace to the uniform, the teachers would say. I didn't care. I was having a great time.

Mrs Tasker didn't like it one bit. She kept me back in class one day to have a 'serious talk' with me.

'Why on earth are you running about with Wizzie?'

'She's my mate,' I said at once.

'Wizzie was never your "mate" as you call her. You fought with her. You never got on with her.'

'I do now, Mrs Tasker. I get on with them all.'

'I don't like it, Hannah. I don't like it at all. And neither do the rest of the teachers.'

'They asked to be friends with me.'

'You could have had other friends, Hannah.'

But I couldn't. Nobody wanted me. Why hadn't she seen that?

'They're trouble, Hannah. These girls are not your type.' I knew she meant they were common, came from the wrong side of town. I had thought that once too. But not any more. 'I think they're good friends, Mrs Tasker.'

She tried one last time to get through to me. Make me drop them. 'There's still a question mark hanging over them about the old woman who was held up. You haven't forgotten her, have you?'

Of course, I hadn't forgotten her. It was the one thing that worried me and I was trying to pluck up the courage to ask them about her too.

It was only a matter of time before my mum found out about my new friends.

She came charging in one night from late-night shopping and dropped her bags with a crash. A bag of frozen peas burst open and scattered noisily on to the kitchen floor.

'What's wrong?' I asked.

'I've just met your friend Erin's mother.' As soon as she said that I knew exactly what was wrong. The cat, as they say, was out of the bag.

She went on. 'At least I thought she was your friend.' She looked at me as if she really wanted to throttle me. 'Why didn't you tell me? I made a real fool of myself. I walked right up to her and said, "Oh, I'm so glad the girls have made up."' When Mum told a story she always put on a posh voice. '"I knew they wouldn't fall out for long," I says to her. And she says to me in that nippy voice of hers, "I don't know who your daughter's made up with, but it certainly wasn't my Erin. I wouldn't let Erin anywhere near her after what she did."'

I got to my feet. 'She said that!'

Mum wasn't listening. 'But she knew exactly who my daughter had made up with, didn't she?! "I think your daughter's found her own class at last, from what Erin tells me." That's what she said to me.' Mum took a deep breath. 'Hannah, what does she mean? Who are you going out with at night?'

But I could tell Mum knew the answer already. Erin's mum and her nippy voice had told her. 'You're going about with that awful Wizzie's gang. I can't believe it. I won't have it, do you hear me? I won't have it.'

223

Now it was my turn to sigh. 'You'll not have what, Mum?'

'I'll not have you going round with that lot.'

'I've been going around with them for a couple of weeks now, Mum, and I haven't got into any trouble.'

She shook her head so violently I was waiting to see it spin across the room. 'It's only a matter of time.'

'So what am I supposed to do, Mum? They're the only friends I've got now.'

She slapped her head dramatically. 'How sad are you? They're the only friends you can get? You must be desperate.'

'I was,' I reminded her.

'Well, you won't be seeing them again. I forbid it. I'll ground you.'

'You can't ground me. I've not done anything wrong!'

She ranted on until I couldn't listen any more. She was going to ground me till I was sixteen, she yelled at me. But I knew she couldn't ground me at all. The way her shifts worked, half the time she wasn't home at night. I'd never really defied her before – never had to with the Lip Gloss Girls. Everything Erin did was just fine, according to my mum. But I would defy her now.

I strode into my room and slammed the door shut. Then I texted them all.

HELP. CRAZY MOTHER.

Wizzie's answer made me laugh.

W8 TILL U MEET MINE. SHE DFNITLY FLU OVR THE CUCU NEST.

I didn't care if it made my mother mad, or if the teachers were annoyed. So Erin's mum thought I'd sunk low. So the teachers thought I was running with a bad crowd. Why should I care what they thought? For the first time in ages, I was enjoying myself. And I hadn't been in a fight once with the Hell Cats. Why couldn't anyone else see that?

CHAPTER FORTY-ONE

Lauren suggested we all meet at her house next night. It was Mum's night for her aerobics class, so she wouldn't be in till later. I'd be back before she was.

I'd never been to any of their houses before. All I knew was that they lived on one of the worst estates in the town. Half the houses were derelict, windows boarded up with steel shutters, yobs running wild, causing chaos. The local paper was always full of stories about the place. I took the train from the station at the top of my street and two stops later I was in another world. I was a little afraid even venturing on to the platform.

'Just wear a bulletproof vest and carry a gun and you should be OK,' Wizzie had warned me on the phone, trying to be funny. I didn't laugh. If I'd had a bulletproof vest it would have been on me. 'That's why everybody's got a Rottweiler up here,' she went on. 'Or keeps a baseball bat behind the door. Safety precaution.'

But Lauren's house was a total surprise. Set in a little cul-de-sac, it was a two-storey semi-detached council house that her parents had bought. The windows sparkled clean and the lights inside were warm and welcoming. The garden was tidy too and well kept, except for an army of garden gnomes. Erin would have laughed at that, called it 'common'. I thought they were kind of cute.

Lauren's mother opened the door and I could see right away where Lauren got her fashion sense from. Her mother's hair was tied up on top of her head with a multi-coloured scarf, and she was wearing some kind of flowery top, tight jeans and orange slippers. She had a wooden spoon in her hand as if she was in the middle of cooking something. Lauren came hurrying downstairs as I came in.

Her mother swung round as Lauren tapped her on the shoulder. Then Lauren started signing to her.

'I'm telling her if she's cooking something we don't want it,' Lauren explained to me. 'She always manages to drop in some strange ingredient – thinks it makes it taste better. It never does.'

Her mother hit her with the spoon. Lauren grabbed

at her head as if she was in pain, and her mother began signing at such a speed I had to laugh. Lauren laughed too.

'Oh, shut up, Mum. You talk such a load of rubbish!' Her mother kept signing away. Lauren turned to me. 'Honestly, see when she starts with those hands of hers, you can't get her to shut up.'

Her dad appeared on the scene then, still in his working clothes. He was a plumber, Lauren had told me. 'What's all this noise?' he said, though there was complete silence. It made me giggle. He winked at me. 'Never marry a woman that talks as much as this! Get in that kitchen, woman, and make me a cup of tea!'

He grabbed Lauren's mum by the shoulder and she started hitting him with the spoon. Tapping him really. He pretended to be mortally hurt, clutched at his arm and shouted, 'Domestic abuse! Call the police!'

It was so crazy I couldn't stop myself laughing.

'They're mad, Hannah. I should have warned you.'

We managed finally to escape to Lauren's room. The rest had already arrived and were lolling about on Lauren's bed. She shared the room with her sister – the one who had been the waitress at the wedding, Ellen. She was getting ready to go out, slipping on a coat. She smiled a greeting to me as I came in. If she knew I'd suspected her, she didn't show it. She told us all to have a nice night, talking in that thick way that deaf people have. 'She makes Mother Teresa look like Adolf Hitler,' I remembered Wizzie telling me. I felt ashamed. How could I have suspected her?

Lauren's room was a dream. The bedcovers and the curtains matched, pale green and cream.

'Mum made them,' she told me when I remarked on how nice they were. 'She's really handy. She made them for Grace as well.'

'So your mother thinks we're beneath you?' Wizzie said, bouncing on the bed, not caring about how creamy the covers were.

'Scum, I think she called you.'

'So glad we've got a good reputation,' she said.

Lauren's mother popped her head in the door and started signing again. Lauren shook her head furiously.

'What was that about?' I asked.

'She's asking if we want some cheese on toast.'

Cheese on toast sounded nice to me. But the rest of them groaned. Wizzie pretended to be sick under the bed.

'It can't be that bad,' I said.

'The last time she made us cheese on toast, she sliced some oranges into it "to add flavour", she said.' Grace shivered at the memory. 'It added something, but it certainly wasn't flavour.'

The wind suddenly howled through the trees outside.

Lauren sat on the floor. 'Who says we'll play Light as a Feather? It's a brilliant night for it.'

You could have knocked me down with one. 'You play that too?'

'Thought it would be too scary for the Lip Gloss Girls,' Wizzie said.

'Bet you don't get it to work,' Sonya said.

'Every time,' I told them.

'Bet your ghost stories are all about little girls screaming and running away from bad people and having handsome hunks save them,' Wizzie said. And she began screaming like a tiny baby.

'You'd never beat me with a ghost story,' I said. A challenge, and I was always up for a challenge.

The room was in darkness and the ghost stories began. Wizzie was first – liked to be first in everything, I suppose. Her story was all slash and blood and horror, about a headless zombie cannibal that kept chasing everybody and eating them. It didn't so much scare you as make you sick.

'How could it chase you if it didn't have a head?' Grace wanted to know. 'It would keep bumping into things, wouldn't it?'

Wizzie rolled her eyes. 'It's a story, Grace. It doesn't have to be logical. Anyway, how would it eat people if it didn't have a head either! You've just got to use your imagination.'

That made us all giggle, except Grace, still trying to work it out.

Sonya told a vampire story, not very well, and Grace's story was so mixed up she forgot the ending. Then it was my turn. I began the video story, speaking in a soft voice, full of atmosphere. I wanted them to know that I was the master storyteller, just as I had been with Erin. I drew them in, told them of the figure in the fog striding towards the shack, even mentioning Mary Brown, a real name, a real girl. I had them mesmerised, listening to my every word. I had almost reached the climax . . .

'Then, I heard the back door of the video shop creak open . . .'

All of a sudden a cupboard door in Lauren's room

flew open, and a dark hooded figure leapt out.

Total panic! We all screamed, fell back in complete confusion. Grace was almost out of the window. Sonya was under the bed. I grabbed a lamp, ready to hurl it at whatever demon was attacking us.

'What's that?!'

'Blinkin' hell, the story come to life.'

Lauren jumped to her feet, switched on the light. The hooded figure whipped off his mask with a flourish.

It was Lauren's dad.

He was laughing so much I thought he was about to burst. 'Gotya, lassies!'

Lauren threw a cushion at him. 'Dad! That could have been fatal!'

'Where did he come from?' I asked.

In answer, her dad, still chuckling away, opened the cupboard door he had leapt from and stepped inside. He pushed another door that opened on to the landing in the hallway. 'Gotya!' he said again. 'Nobody ever remembers I can get in from the landing that way! Especially on a dark night . . . with the lights off, and the wind blowing.' He began to howl like a wolf.

Grace flopped on to the bed. 'See you, Mr Winters!'

She said it as if Lauren's dad always got up to tricks like that.

I hadn't laughed like that in so long. And here I was laughing again with the Hell Cats.

Curiouser and curiouser.

CHAPTER FORTY-TWO

Light as a Feather was forgotten. The mood gone. Even the wind had died down.

Lauren put on her music and we all began singing along with our favourite tunes. Wizzie was leaping about on the bed. I waited for Lauren to tell her to stop, but no one said a word to her. I'd like to see my mum allowing that!

Then I stopped singing. I listened. One of us had a beautiful voice, and it certainly wasn't me.

I looked at Lauren.

She looked back at me. Stopped singing too. 'What?'

'You're a really good singer,' I said.

'You don't have to sound so surprised.'

'She is, isn't she?' Wizzie said, flopping on the bed at last. She said it as if it was something they had told Lauren lots of times. 'Her brother's got a band. When she's older she's going to sing in it. We're always telling her to go for auditions.'

But I had a much better idea. 'Why don't you go in for the school show? They're doing *Grease*. You'd make a great Sandy.'

Lauren looked at me as if I had two heads. 'Me?'

'Well, we know you can be a Pink Lady.'

Grace interrupted. 'What's a Pink Lady? Is that not some kind of cocktail?'

'The Pink Ladies is the name of the girl gang in the film,' I told her. 'They're rough and tough and common . . . a bit like us.'

Wizzie grimaced. 'And they call themselves the Pink Ladies? That's really rough and tough, that is.'

I ignored her. I turned to Lauren. 'I think you might brush up quite well and be a Sandy. Sandy's the sweet and innocent one that ends up in the Pink Ladies.'

Now they all laughed.

'Lauren, sweet and innocent!' Wizzie threw herself back onto the bed, holding her stomach, killing herself laughing. 'That's a good one!'

'What's *Grease*?' It was Grace who asked.

'*Grease*, the film. The musical. You must have seen it.' I burst into song. 'Summer Lovin'. Everybody knows that song. Even my out-of-tune version.

Grace nodded at last. 'Oh aye, I remember that one.'

'Wonderful film,' I went on. 'Olivia Newton Mearns and John Revoltin' are in it.'

Wizzie's chewing gum flew out of her mouth. Lauren swallowed hers. Sonya fell off the bed.

Grace just looked blank. 'Aye, right!' she snapped at me. 'His name's not John Revoltin'. You're winding me up.'

'And her name's not Newton Mearns either, Grace. Newton Mearns is a small town near Glasgow.'

Wizzie threw a pillow at me. 'Show off!'

I smiled at Grace. Didn't want to annoy her. I was still trying to win her round, but honestly, sometimes it was such fun winding her up.

Sonya flopped beside Wizzie. 'Whoever heard of one of us getting a part in the school show? The teachers hate us.'

Lauren shrugged. 'What would be the point of going for an audition?'

Wizzie stood up. 'Aye, what would be the point? Whoever heard of a Hell Cat trying for the school show?'

'Yeah,' Grace agreed. 'Would never happen.'

'Never want it to happen. School show's for muppets.'

If there was a real edge in Wizzie's voice, I must have missed it. Maybe I was too excited at what I was already planning. I knew I couldn't let this pass. This just had to happen.

I made sure I was last to leave Lauren's that night.

'You've got to promise me you'll go in for the school show, Lauren.'

She stood at the door and shook her head. 'Me? They'd never give the part to me.'

All Lauren needed, I was sure, was a little bit of persuasion. I'd be there to give that. 'But you're a great singer. I've never heard anybody sing as well as you.'

And I hadn't. Not even Rose. She thought the part was hers. She was sure of it. We all were.

Now I intended different. And wouldn't that be sweet revenge on Rose?

CHAPTER FORTY-THREE

It felt as if Lauren and I had been friends all our lives.

I went to her house often after that first night, doing my very best to persuade her to audition for the show. I knew I was doing it behind Wizzie's back, but Wizzie was so set against it. 'We're not the Lip Gloss Girls, you know,' she would say whenever I mentioned it. So I stopped mentioning it in front of her.

I loved going to Lauren's. Everybody was welcomed here, even Wizzie. I loved the way her family all joked with each other. It was like walking into a comedy show every time I went there. It was the quietest house I had ever been in, yet it never felt like that. It always seemed to be filled with chatter and laughing. Why couldn't I have fun like that with my mum? I said as much to Lauren one night.

'I don't think you give your mum a chance,' Lauren said. 'You're always that serious about her.'

'That's because she's always so serious. She's always going on about being such a loser, nothing ever going right for her. She depresses me. She makes me feel like a loser too.'

'You! You've got to be joking. I used to see you with Erin and them, and you were so full of it. Thought you were something. And you're trying to tell me you felt like a loser?'

And I remembered how confident I always felt with the Lip Gloss Girls. Sure of myself because I had my friends around me. 'Is that how I really looked to you?'

'You better believe it. That's why none of us liked you. But it's funny when you think about it, Hannah. I used to hate you, and now that I've got to know you . . . you and I get on really well, don't we?'

Who would have thought it? I remembered the fights I'd had with Lauren, the way I'd slagged off her hair, and her clothes, the insults she'd traded with me. Now, when I didn't come to her house, we phoned each other at least ten times a night. Never ran out of things to talk about.

Lauren went on. 'Do you know what else I think is funny? I want to be just like my mum. And you want to be the exact opposite of yours.'

'Can you blame me?'

'I've never met your mum, but do you know what I think about her from things you tell me?'

I didn't want to hear this, so sure she was going to say something negative. Erin always had something negative to say about my mum. 'I'd rather have my teeth drilled without anaesthetic than have a mum like yours,' she had once told me. I should have known better with Lauren.

She went on, 'Your mum seems to be somebody who's always trying to better herself. You're always telling us she's going to classes for this and that. Spanish, and painting, and aerobics.'

'Trying to make up for not having friends probably.' I regretted saying that right away. *Just as bad as my mum*, I thought.

Lauren obviously thought the same thing. 'That's a really rotten thing to say. You told me your mum always looks for the worst in people. Well, so do you. You've just done it with your mum.'

She was so right about that. I felt guilty. 'I wish I knew how to make her happy, Lauren. I could never understand why she did what she did.'

Lauren knew about my mum. Didn't everybody in

the town know? I didn't have to explain what I meant.

'They say it's a cry for help.'

A cry for help. 'I understand that now.' I didn't tell Lauren why I understood that. And Lauren didn't ask. I could talk to her about everything, except that. That would always be my secret, a secret never to be told. There are some secrets you should never share. Perhaps that had been Erin's mistake, sharing her secret with anyone.

'Anyway, when am I going to meet her?' Lauren asked.

None of them had ever been to my house. I'd never had the nerve to invite them. And though she couldn't keep me in, and didn't really try, she still moaned constantly at me for going around with the Hell Cats. I knew it worried her.

'Are you ashamed of us or something?' Lauren asked.

I giggled. 'Maybe a bit.'

'Your mum still not trust us, eh? But she must see you've never been in any trouble since you've gone about with us, have you? We haven't even been in any fights.' She giggled. 'Mind you, the only ones we ever had real fights with were you lot . . . the Lip Gloss Girls.'

That made me laugh. 'We were the same,' I said. 'We'd do all the things you do, march along the water-front, daring the other girls to break us up. They never did. We had a reputation because we were always in fights with you.' I began to laugh. 'How crazy is that!'

'See, the Hell Cats are just a nice bunch of girls really.' She pouted and fluttered her eyelashes.

I laughed too, until I remembered the cloud hanging over the Hell Cats, and the old woman.

'There's something I have to ask you.' Now, I decided, was as good a time as any. Now, when it was just me and Lauren. I wouldn't have had the nerve if Wizzie had been there. 'What about the old woman?'

'You don't really think we had anything to do with that?'

'The police questioned you. They came to the school.'

'There's lots of girl gangs on this estate,' Lauren said. 'You've seen some of them. The police never seriously thought it was us. They questioned lots of girls.'

'It was because of the knife, wasn't it?'

Lauren looked genuinely puzzled. 'What knife?'

'Everybody knows Wizzie carries a knife.'

She dismissed that with a wave of her hand. 'Have

242

you ever seen Wizzie with a knife?'

'But the scars . . .'

Lauren didn't say anything for a moment. 'Wizzie lives in the worst part of this estate. Even I'm not allowed to go to her house. Her family have got a really bad reputation and there are some really bad gangs round her way. You've seen the worst of them, the Black Widows. I think that's where she gets the scars. She's in fights with other gangs. But she won't tell us about it. There's a lot of things Wizzie doesn't tell us.'

'Now that I've met you, I wonder why you're so friendly with Wizzie,' I said. 'You're so different.'

'Wizzie and I have been mates since primary school. Wizzie was always trying to be tough. But my mum likes Wizzie. She worries about her – so do I. If she didn't have me . . .' Lauren thought about that. 'If she didn't have us . . . I'm scared she would end up in one of those other gangs.'

'Do you think that could happen?'

Lauren nodded. 'I think she tries to impress them, show she's every bit as tough as they are. But she's not really. She's a softie.'

Wizzie a softie? No, I decided then. That I would never believe.

CHAPTER FORTY-FOUR

Only a couple of nights later, Lauren appeared at my house. She had obviously decided the time to meet my mum was now. I nearly had a heart attack when I opened the door to her. Her hair was tied up in three bunches, she was wearing a long multi-coloured cardigan that stretched down to her knees, black tights with holes in them, and a pair of ankle boots.

Typical Lauren, but my mum had never seen her before. What kind of impression was she going to make?

I couldn't take my eyes off the cardigan.

'Like it?' Lauren asked. 'My mum knit it.'

'Is your mum blind as well as deaf?'

That only made Lauren giggle. 'You're terrible, Hannah!'

Mum came into the hall just then, a tray of freshly baked shortbread in her hand. She took one look at Lauren and gaped.

Lauren beamed at her. 'Hello, Mrs Driscoll. I've been looking forward to meeting you.'

I could see my mum didn't quite know how to handle this, so I changed the subject immediately. 'You've made some shortbread, Mum.' I turned to Lauren. 'My mum makes the best shortbread. Try some.'

I took the tray from Mum's hands and held it out to Lauren. Lauren picked a piece, already cut into triangles, and popped half of it in her mouth. 'You're right, Hannah. That is the best shortbread I've ever tasted.'

'I know it is, but Mum doesn't think she's a very good baker.'

'You could sell that.' Lauren looked at me. 'You should take it to the next school fête. Some of the baking people bring would poison you. I don't know how they've got the nerve to try and sell it.'

Mum shrugged. 'I'm sure my shortbread's not that special,' she said, but I could tell she was pleased.

Lauren rattled on. 'My mum gives me baking to take to the school every year. Doesn't know I throw it to the birds as soon as I'm out of the house. Mind you, the birds turn their noses up at it as well. Or should that be their beaks?' She giggled, and I could see Mum wasn't sure how to take that. Lauren saw it too. 'My mum's brilliant, but she's the world's worst baker.' Lauren bit into the other half of the shortbread. 'Maybe you could give her lessons, Mrs Driscoll. Can I have another piece?'

When we were in my room I asked her, 'Is that why you came? So you could suck up to Mum?'

'Maybe I thought it was time I met her. She's nice by the way. She's really pretty.'

I thought about that. She was nice. And she *was* pretty. Always trying to better herself, Lauren had said. And I had never given her any credit for that. Never gave her any credit for anything. Looking after Junior since his mother died, always working hard, always there for me. I felt suddenly ashamed of myself. 'Suppose she is,' I said.

Lauren wandered about my room. 'This is nice. And you've got a room to yourself. Lucky!'

'Are you going to go for the show then?'

Lauren shrugged. 'I'm thinking about it.'

That made me happy. 'While you're thinking about it, you should practise. I've got the *Grease* DVD. Want to see it?'

I pulled it from my rack and slipped it in the machine.

'Just one thing . . .' Lauren said seriously. 'I don't want Wizzie to know – not till I've really decided. OK?'

That was OK by me. I wanted this to be a surprise to everyone. We'd tell Wizzie soon enough, and Grace and Sonya, but as for the rest of the school . . . the first time they found out would be when Lauren paraded into that auditorium, dressed as Sandy.

Halfway through the film, Mum came in with tea and more shortbread, and sandwiches too. She was showing off, and usually it would embarrass and annoy me. But not this time. Lauren had her laughing, telling her about her mother's cooking.

'Please . . . give my mum the recipe for this short-bread.' Then Lauren waved her arms about madly. 'No! Don't bother. She'd probably add one of her strange ingredients . . . anchovies or something.'

'What are you watching?' Mum asked.

'*Grease*,' I said.

'Your daughter thinks I should go for a part in it. Me?' Lauren held up her multi-coloured bunches. 'Can you imagine me!'

'Not *a* part. The main part. She's a brilliant singer, Mum.'

Lauren blushed. 'How could I look like that?' We

had paused the film right at the scene where Olivia Newton John is singing and looking as sweet as an angel.

'I think you should go for it,' Mum said. 'It's amazing what a change of clothes and hair can do. In fact, I'll look out some clothes I've got that just might be useful. Never fit you, of course.'

'My mum's really handy with a needle. She'd fix them.' Lauren laughed. 'You really think I could look like that?'

'Well, they're always doing makeovers on television. Why couldn't you have one?'

And I knew then Lauren would definitely go for the part. Thanks to Mum. They seemed to genuinely like each other!

By the end of that night Lauren had my mum eating out of her hand.

Later, when Lauren had left I went into Mum's room. She was reading her book in bed. I sat beside her. 'Thanks, Mum,' I said. 'For the shortbread and everything.'

She laid down her book. 'She seems a nice girl,' she said.

'She is. They are, they all are.'

She wasn't sure about that. But Lauren had made a difference. Mum liked her. Maybe she was thinking – I was sure of it – that if she met the others, she might like them too.

All except Wizzie.

CHAPTER FORTY-FIVE

Wizzie was a softie, Lauren had told me. That was even harder to believe just a few nights later when we met at the Mall. One more scar, looking raw. 'Were you in another fight?' Lauren asked her.

Wizzie only shrugged. 'Ask me no questions and I'll tell you no lies.'

Wizzie and her scars. Yes, I decided. I would have to pluck up a lot of courage to bring Wizzie home.

We were still laughing when I saw Erin coming out of Top Shop, doing some late-night shopping. She saw me too. She glanced at me, then just as quickly looked away and kept her eyes straight in front of her. My gaze never left her. She was on her own, clutching her bags close. Nervous. It would have been so easy to confront her, to surround her, make her scared the way she'd made me scared. But all I did was stare. She was bold enough, finally, to look back, and there was something in her eyes that looked like hate.

I felt Wizzie's hand on my shoulder. 'Not worth it,' she said.

'I know,' I said. 'But I'm going to get her. I'm going to get them all.'

And I was, one by one.

'And the first one's going to be Rose,' I said. 'I can't wait to see her face when you win that audition, Lauren.' It was out before I could stop myself.

There was a sudden silence. I was still staring at Erin's back as she hurried out of the Mall. I realised at once that I had put my foot right in it. Not just one foot. Both of them. I turned quickly to see Lauren blowing out her cheeks, Grace and Sonya standing back. And Wizzie. She had one hand on her hip, and she was glaring at me.

'What's all this about an audition? I thought that was all forgotten.' She swivelled round to Lauren. 'Are you doing this behind my back?'

She didn't wait for Lauren's answer. She swung right back to me. 'Your idea? Using us to get back at your old pals.' She looked round at them all. 'Come on, can you not see that's what she's doing?'

I saw Lauren swallow before she answered her. 'Well,

we want to get back at them too, Wizzie.'

'So let's start a fight with them. But we don't get them back like this.' She put on a little girlie voice. 'Ooo, we're so bad, we're going to sing better than them.' Her voice became harsh again. 'That's really going to scare them to death, that is.'

'Lauren's a r-really good singer,' Sonya said.

To my surprise it was Grace who spoke out boldly. 'So why shouldn't one of the Hell Cats get a part in their daft show? Lauren's the best singer in the school.'

That only made Wizzie madder. 'So every one of you knows about this . . . except Wizzie. What else are you doing behind my back?'

Lauren tried to protest. But there was nothing any of us could say. Wizzie was right. We had talked about it and decided it behind her back, because we knew this would be her reaction.

Lauren touched her arm and Wizzie pulled away. 'Come on, Wizzie. We knew you wouldn't like the idea . . . I didn't like it at first, but I'm up for it now.'

Wizzie turned on her. 'No, you're not, Lauren. She's making you do it.' She pointed a black-nailed finger at me. 'You wouldn't have thought about it if it wasn't for her.' Then she turned to me and poked her finger into my chest. Her little white face was red with anger. 'You're every bit as manipulative as that Erin.'

That really hurt. 'Don't say that, Wizzie.'

But she wasn't going to stop. 'You're trying to turn us into the Lip Gloss Girls, and I don't like it!'

CHAPTER FORTY-SIX

The night before the auditions we all gathered at Lauren's house. All of us except Wizzie. We waited and waited and she didn't turn up. She'd been annoyed since she'd found out that Lauren was still going to audition, no matter what she said.

'Is Wizzie mad at me?' I asked.

Grace answered. 'I think she's just mad.'

'She'll be fine,' Lauren said. 'She told me today I'd get that part for sure.' Then she laughed. 'Said she'd punch Hammond's lights out if I didn't. She's for it, she just doesn't want to admit it, because it wasn't her idea in the first place.'

But I couldn't help wondering, where was Wizzie? Since the night at the Mall she'd missed a few of our meetings. I kept remembering those horrible Black Widows and hoped she wasn't with them.

What else were we doing behind her back? she had

asked. But I wondered, what else was Wizzie doing behind ours?

'Oh well, her loss,' I said, trying to be cheery.

Lauren's mum brought in toasted cheese sandwiches for our supper. 'I've added some cinnamon and garlic tonight,' she told us, as she brought in a plate piled high. 'I think it brings out the flavour of the cheese.'

'I don't know about bringing it out, but I'm bringing it up in five minutes,' I whispered.

Lauren's brother sent us all a really rude text message that sent us into a fit of giggles. Her dad popped in with funny stories about strange objects that got stuck in drainpipes. Her sister Ellen was all nervous because she was going out on a first date with a new boyfriend. No wonder we always loved coming to Lauren's.

Wizzie wasn't here and I felt we were all more relaxed. We lay along the beds and laughed and fixed our hair, tried on each other's clothes and did all the things I used to do with the Lip Gloss Girls. Maybe Wizzie was right. Without her, we were turning into them.

'I'm really nervous about this daft audition,' Lauren said. 'I don't know why I'm even trying for it.'

'Because *she* said so,' Grace said, giving me a push.

'And it's getting to the stage where we seem to be doing everything she wants.' I looked at her quickly, sure she was getting at me. But there was a smile on her face. Grace was enjoying it too.

'You'll be brilliant,' I told Lauren – couldn't have her backing out now.

Lauren took one look in her mirror. 'Look at me. This Sandy is supposed to be sweet and innocent.' She held out her topsy-turvy hair. 'I look like a scarecrow. I'm a mess. How am I ever going to convince anybody I could be Sandy?'

'My mum's told me exactly how to do your hair tomorrow. It'll be fine.'

'Or you could just shave your head,' Sonya suggested. 'You'd look great in the school play bald.'

The idea seemed to appeal to Lauren. 'Hey, do you think that would look funky?'

'That's what I love about you, Lauren,' Sonya said. 'You've got the guts to be different. You would shave your head just to see what it looked like!'

'And that's what I really like about you,' I said, suddenly wanting them all to know how I felt. 'About the whole lot of you.' I looked around at them. Sonya, with the stutter; Grace, who never got a joke and with her long horsey face (well, let's face it – that's the only way you could describe her); Lauren, with her idiot hair-styles. And I thought about Wizzie, with her rings and her scars. 'I like how you are all different, and you bump each other up all the time.'

They all looked at me as if I'd said something really stupid. 'I hope you don't expect a group hug next,' Grace said solemnly.

'Not like your old pals,' Sonya said.

I felt so far away from those 'old pals' now, as if all that belonged in another world.

'No,' I said. Me and my 'old pals' hadn't wanted to be different. I could see that now. We had all wanted to be the same. We had all wanted to be like Erin.

Erin. I hated her more at that moment than I ever had before.

'You've got them back anyway. You're one of us now.'

I was, and I was glad of it. But it wasn't enough. Not by a long way.

'It's going to be the icing on the cake when Lauren gets that part tomorrow. I'm dying to see their faces!'

The thought of the audition set Lauren off in moans and sighs once again. 'What am I doing this for? I'm so nervous.'

'You will get the part.' I was sure of it. Mr Hammond was a fair man. He would give the part to the best singer, and that was Lauren. Anyway, he'd never had any time for the Lip Gloss Girls either.

I lay in bed that night and I couldn't get to sleep. Thinking over everything, thinking especially about Erin.

Manipulative. The word repeated itself over and over in my head. That was Erin. Manipulating me, manipulating us all. She'd made a fool of my mum, and I had let her. She'd made a fool of Heather that night at the wedding, and I had laughed too. Why had I never realised that before?

My mobile rang at midnight. It was Lauren. 'I can't sleep, Hannah. I'm dead nervous. What am I doing this for? They'll all laugh at me.'

'Because you want to,' I told her. 'And because you're good. It'll be a laugh. And I'll be there with you.'

After I'd spoken to her I snuggled down under the duvet. I was filled with a warm feeling of friendship for Lauren. Who would ever have thought that? I'd once thought she was hard and tough and common. And here she was, phoning me because she was nervous about an audition for a school musical. Had she phoned any of the others? I hoped she hadn't. I wanted to be Lauren's friend. Anyway, I didn't think she had. It was me she'd turned to. I was nervous too. She just had to get that part. It would bug Rose so much if she did.

It had been a good night. One of those nights you imagine you're going to remember for the rest of your life.

But where had Wizzie been? Was she annoyed because Lauren was going in for the school musical? Annoyed at me? Was she moving away from us towards one of those other gangs? The Black Widows?

It was as I was drifting off to sleep that I realised there was something else. Something kept repeating itself in my head. Something that I was sure was significant. Something about Wizzie.

Everyone's got secrets, Wizzie had said that first night we went to the Mall . . . and I wondered, what was Wizzie's secret?

CHAPTER FORTY-SEVEN

The auditions were to take place after school. No one knew that Lauren was going in for the part of Sandy. No one would ever expect one of us to even consider such a thing. It had to be a complete surprise to everyone. I had decided that we were going to make an entrance. My mum had sorted out Lauren's wardrobe for the audition and Lauren's mum had fixed the clothes so they were just right for her. After school we headed for the girls' toilets to change. Lauren and I went into one of the cubicles while the others waited outside.

Wizzie stood guard at the door, to stop anyone else from coming in.

'Better use the toilets on the bottom floor,' she told a couple of girls who tried to get in. 'Sonya's got a bad case of diarrhoea in here.'

Sonya almost screeched. 'What did you tell them that for? Why me?'

Wizzie only shrugged. 'Had to tell them something, didn't I? Nobody'll want into this lavvy now.'

In the cubicle, I brushed and brushed at Lauren's hair, just the way Mum had shown me. I pulled it back into a ponytail and held it with a ribbon. I had brought wipes and by the time I'd finished, Lauren's face was shining, and so was her hair. Lauren was really pretty, I thought, and once she put on the soft pink skirt and the blouse my mum had supplied her with I was really amazed at the change in her. She stepped out of the cubicle like a model at a fashion show.

'Tara!'

It wasn't just me who gasped. Grace almost swallowed her chewing gum. Sonya shrieked. Wizzie drew in her breath.

'What do you think?' Lauren said. She saw all their astonished faces. 'Do you think I look daft?'

Sonya suddenly burst out laughing. 'You were born to wear a ponytail.'

'You look just like her in the film,' Grace said.

I laughed. 'She means Olivia Newton Mearns.'

Grace giggled. We all did. The only one who wasn't laughing was Wizzie. She was leaning on the wall, watching Lauren sullenly.

'What's wrong with your face?' I asked her.

'She definitely looks like one of the Lip Gloss Girls now.'

I could see what she meant. Lauren did. The fierceness had come from that wild hair of hers, and her crazy clothes. This was a different Lauren. She looked sweet and innocent. She had the fresh face of a cherub, scrubbed and rosy cheeked.

'Weird what a change of hair can do, or clothes,' Sonya said.

'Or a good wash,' I added, and Lauren gave me a push that sent me flying.

'I'm sure I can remember having a bath once,' she said.

Wizzie might not have liked it, but she was a mate. She linked her arm in Lauren's and we marched along the corridor together towards the auditorium, striding it out, with Lauren in the middle of us.

'I hope you know we haven't a hope,' Wizzie said. 'Everybody hates us.' Then she grinned. 'Who says we'll trash the place if she doesn't get the part?'

What an entrance we made. Wizzie pushed through the double doors, making such a clatter I was sure the doors were coming off their hinges.

I walked after her, with Grace and Sonya. We left Lauren to glide in behind us, like a queen. Everyone turned to look. I clocked them. There was big Anil, folded over a seat – probably didn't even have to audition, big show-off. Zak Riley was there too. Surely he didn't expect a part? But the ones my eyes searched out – the only ones I was interested in – were Erin and co. They were right at the front, no surprise there, and Erin got to her feet to watch us. She stood rigid, the way she always did when she was spoiling for a fight. The rest stood up too and turned to look at us.

Wizzie held up her hands. 'It's OK. No applause. Not at the moment. Autographs later.'

We took our seats at the back and spread ourselves out. Mr Hammond hurried towards us. 'What are you doing here? You better not be here to cause trouble.'

'Us, sir?' I said, all innocence.

'We're here to audition.' He stared at Wizzie when she said that, disbelief written all over his face in big letters. Don't know why he looked so surprised. Seeing her sitting there, with her wild hair and her eyebrow pierced, I thought she would have made a great Rizzo, the leader of the Pink Ladies.

'Don't worry,' Wizzie said. 'I'm not going into your

daft play.' She pulled at Lauren's pink cardigan. 'She is.'

Mr Hammond's eyes travelled to Lauren, all pink and fresh and pretty, and stayed there, as if he was trying to figure out if he knew her. 'My goodness, Lauren, I wouldn't have recognised you. I didn't know you could sing.'

'Wait till you hear her,' I said. 'Hidden talents.'

He turned his attention to me then. 'Ah, so this is your doing. And what part is Lauren auditioning for?' He was asking me, not Lauren. I could almost see Lauren ready to say she'd take anything, but I was having none of that.

'The main part. Sandy. That's the only one she's interested in.'

His eyes narrowed. 'I see,' he said.

'You'll give her a fair shot at it, won't you, sir?'

Mr Hammond didn't think Lauren stood a chance. None of them did. He still thought we were here for a laugh, to make a complete mess of his audition. 'Of course I will. But I'll be keeping my eye on you,' he said, and then he hurried back down to the front of the stage.

It would have been hard not to make a fool of the auditions. How some people have the nerve to get up and sing beats me.

The boys were first. And that was such a laugh. Everyone knew the main part would go to big Anil. He didn't even need to sing. But he did, just so the girls could swoon at him.

Another couple of boys tried out for the same part, but they didn't stand a chance.

There were no surprises when Mr Hammond announced that Anil would play the lead. I called up to the teacher, 'Cheat! He was definitely miming, sir!'

Almost everyone laughed, even big Anil. Only the Lip Gloss Girls kept their faces straight and solemn. And Mr Hammond. He shook his head in a warning, still sure we were here to make trouble.

Zak Riley got a part too, as one of the more stupid members of the gang. 'Type casting!' I called up when we heard that news.

Then it was the girls' turn, and that was even funnier. Mary Fortune got up and belted out 'Simply the Best' as if she was Tina Turner herself. She was awful. We stamped and whistled when she'd finished as if she'd been brilliant. She knew we were making a fool of her and glared daggers at us. She was so busy glaring she tripped and fell off the stage. That only made us whistle and cheer even louder. Mr Hammond came up and warned us to shut up. 'I'll put you out if there's any more of that.'

Lauren whispered as he walked away, 'I'm definitely not getting that part now.'

She looked nervous. Little bubbles of sweat dotted her top lip. I glanced at Rose. She didn't look nervous at all. Confidence oozed from her. I could see Erin and the new girl, Geraldine Mooney, whispering in her ear, probably telling her how wonderful she was going to be. They would be sure she would walk this one. So had I, once.

Until I had heard Lauren sing.

Eventually, it was Rose's turn. She stood up, smiling, and walked straight-backed to the stage. Erin and the rest started cheering and stamping and whistling, just as we had done, but Mr Hammond didn't rush to silence them.

And Rose started to sing 'Summer Lovin'.

Lauren turned to me. 'That's the song I'm going to sing!'

I grinned at her. 'I know. But you'll sing it better.'

And she would.

Rose was a good singer, can't take that away from her. She could carry a tune, she kept time. I have to

266

admit she even looked pretty. But there was nothing special about her voice, nothing at all. I could tell that now, now that I had heard Lauren. Mr Hammond wandered around the auditorium as he listened, finally standing right at the back.

Then she was done. Everyone applauded apart from Erin and the rest, who went wild.

Lauren leant across to me. 'I think she already has the part. I'm going home.' She was ready to stand up and leave and I could understand why. Even Mr Hammond was clapping and he hadn't done that with anyone else.

'Lovely, Rose. Thank you.' It was almost as if he had made up his mind too.

I gripped Lauren's hand, squeezed it. 'It's Lauren's turn now, sir.'

He turned towards us and his smile disappeared. But if there was something I could say about Mr Hammond, it was that he was fair – one of those teachers who always tries to do the right thing. I just hoped he wasn't going to let me down now.

'OK, Lauren. On you come.' Then his beady eye settled on me once again. 'And this had better not be a joke, Hannah.'

I realised then that he thought Lauren was going to be deliberately rubbish, and the whole audition would end in chaos. In fact, when I looked around I knew that was what they all thought. They weren't interested in Lauren's singing at all. Some were slumped on seats, talking, or flicking through magazines. If they were watching it was only because they were ready for a laugh.

Lauren almost tripped on to the stage and that sent Erin off, whistling again.

'Go for it, Lauren!' I called out from the back, just to let her know we were all there for her, no matter what.

And Lauren started to sing, and then they all listened.

Boy, did they listen. They stopped riffling through magazines, they all shut up, they all watched her. No one had ever heard her sing before. I had never heard her sing so well. Just a few bars in and Lauren forgot her nerves. Her voice carried right to the back of the auditorium and as Mr Hammond wandered up and stood behind us, I knew he was impressed with that too. And Lauren didn't just sing. She moved with the music, her face animated, singing as if she meant every word.

People started clapping, swaying with the rhythm, joining in the chorus – really enjoying the song. They hadn't done that with Rose. I knew then that if Lauren didn't get that part it would be a total cheat.

When she'd finished everyone was silent. Lauren blinked and looked round the auditorium, wondering why no one was clapping her. It was big Anil who clapped first. This was his leading lady. And he liked it. And then everyone in the auditorium erupted, whistling, cheering, stamping feet. Lauren blushed and smiled. Wizzie slunk down further in her seat. 'Now she really does look like a Lip Gloss Girl.' But she wasn't smiling about it.

Mr Hammond had to shut everyone up. The only ones who didn't applaud were Erin and the rest. A rage hung over them like a wet blanket.

Mr Hammond strode to the front of the stage, still clapping.

'Was that all right, sir?' Lauren asked.

'That was better than all right, Lauren,' he said. 'Where have you been hiding yourself?' Lauren looked out towards us. 'It was Hannah's idea. She heard me sing and said I should try out for this.'

Then he turned, looked directly at me. 'Ah, so you

only discovered you could sing since you've been in Hannah's gang.'

I felt Wizzie stiffen beside me. Hannah's gang. Not Wizzie's. She didn't like that.

But I did.

Hannah's gang.

Mr Hammond consulted his flip chart where he'd been jotting down notes all through the auditions. 'Well, you've all been wonderful, but I think we've found our Sandy.' And he stepped forward and held out his hand to Lauren. 'Congratulations.'

The place went wild. We leapt on to the seats, cheering and shouting. It was a great moment, especially when I watched Erin and Rose, almost in tears, run from the auditorium. Rose turned to me at the door. I'd never seen her so angry. Her heart had been set on this part. She'd been sure it was in her pocket. And Lauren had won it over her. Good.

Let her be angry. I wanted her angry and disappointed and hurt. Let her stew.

This was my great moment, and I was going to enjoy it.

CHAPTER FORTY-EIGHT

I wasn't surprised to find them all waiting for us when we strode out of the auditorium. Lauren had been kept back by Mr Hammond so we were outnumbered. Not a problem. Everyone else had cleared off. They knew trouble was coming.

'You bitch!' Erin screeched at me, and before I could think of a good answer she ran at me and brought her nails down my face. 'You did this on purpose.' The fury of her assault had taken me by surprise. My face stung.

'I can't help it if Lauren's a better singer than pudding face there.'

Rose was ready to run at me when I said that. 'You knew that was my song!'

'I only knew you were going to murder it.' I looked round at my mates. 'Can you get charged with murdering a song?' Rose really did leap at me then.

It was Sonya to the rescue. 'Get your paws off my mate.'

Erin pulled Rose away from me. 'With pleasure. She might catch something if I don't. Anyway, you can have her. She's got what she deserves at last.'

I was right in her face. 'Yeah, I deserve the best. And that's what I've got.'

'I hate you, Hannah Driscoll.' Erin said it through her gritted teeth. 'Hate you.'

'I hate you as well.' Rose's eyes were filled to the brim with tears.

Wizzie had had enough. She spat on the ground, pushed at Rose's shoulder. 'Are you snivelling because you lost a part in the school musical? What a wimp.' She turned her back on Rose and laughed. 'She wants to get a life, eh?'

She hardly got the words out of her mouth. Rose leapt on her back, tried to claw at her face – took Wizzie so much by surprise she was pulled down. Then Erin was on me again, and I was going down for nobody. She reached out to punch me and I caught her wrist and twisted it up her back. She yelled and kicked me hard on the shins but even that didn't make me let her go. 'Thought you could drag me down, Erin, and

I'd never get up? Well, I did, and look who's on top now . . . and don't think I've finished with you yet . . . I'm coming to get you.'

'LET HER GO!'

Mrs Tasker's voice boomed down the corridor. She ran at us, grabbing me by the collar, yanking me away from Erin. 'Did you just threaten Erin there, Hannah?'

'She did, Mrs Tasker. She's a witch.' Erin pulled herself away from me.

'Takes one to know one.'

Mrs Tasker already had Wizzie by the arm. 'All of you are coming with me to the headmaster.'

'We've got season tickets for his office,' I said cheekily.

We were practically frogmarched to the office. Mr McGinty railed at us. 'You're worse than boys when you get started.'

Did he think that was an insult? We loved hearing that. Worse than boys.

It was me he was singling out. 'I'd have thought you'd had enough of gangs, Hannah. Now you seem to have taken over from Wizzie.'

I'd taken over from Wizzie? Was that what they all thought? Wizzie shuffled beside me. It was getting to her, I could tell that.

Lauren was waiting for us at the gates when we all came out, anxious to hear what had happened.

But she hardly listened really. She had lots to tell us too. She was more excited than I'd ever seen her. 'There's going to be loads of rehearsals. I'll hardly ever see you lot.'

'You're going to be brilliant,' I told her.

'Do you get to kiss big Anil?' was all Grace wanted to know.

Lauren laughed. 'Don't think old Hammond approves of kissing. But I might just jump him anyway. You know how us actresses like to improvise.' Then she stopped and grabbed me. 'Thanks, Hannah. I'd never have done that without you.'

Sonya patted me on the back. 'Good one, Hannah. Did you see the look on Erin's face?'

'And that wimp, Rose, crying. I'd pay money to see that again.' Even Grace approved.

The only one who wasn't laughing was Wizzie. She was standing back, watching me.

'Are you OK, Wizzie?'

She didn't look OK. She was angry, I could tell. I couldn't blame her really. Her friends were all crowded round me as if I was the leader, as if I had taken over from her.

Wizzie stood apart from us, glaring at me. And it scared me.

CHAPTER FORTY-NINE

Over the next few days we hardly saw Lauren. She was always at rehearsals for the show. Even during break times she seemed to spend more time with the other members of the cast, waving to us in the canteen, or grinning at us whenever she went by. I'd see her with big Anil, as he bent down to talk to her. 'Do you think he fancies Lauren?' Grace asked one day.

'I only think he fancies himself,' I said. But I began to wonder. Lauren looked so different. She always seemed to look clean and fresh. She even came in to school one day wearing a pale blue sweater. That made Wizzie really mad.

'What's all this about?!' She plucked at the sweater. 'Pastel shades and a ponytail? Have you been taken over by the bodysnatchers?'

And I remembered Wizzie's words – I was turning them into the Lip Gloss Girls.

We seemed to be seeing less of Wizzie too. In the evenings she sometimes didn't come to the Mall. Me and Sonya and Grace would meet up, but not Wizzie.

'She wasn't in when I phoned her,' Sonya would say.

But she never answered when any of us phoned her. Phone always turned off.

'I'm worried about her,' I told them.

It was my mother who surprised me most. 'I'm so happy about Lauren getting that part,' she said. 'You must get me tickets to see that show.' Was Lauren turning into the next Erin? I hoped not.

'I see Erin Brodie's still mad at you,' Wizzie said one day in the canteen when we caught Erin doing her glaring act at me.

'She's waiting for me to get her,' I said. 'Well, she'll have to wait.'

'As long as she doesn't have to wait too long,' Wizzie said. 'Then she might think you're talking through your hat.'

There was something in that. So as Erin walked past our table I called out to her, 'Don't worry, I haven't forgotten about you . . . I'm still going to get you.'

Everyone heard me. They turned to watch, waiting

for me to 'get her' right now. Waiting for me to jump at her, start a fight.

Sonya was ready to do just that, but I held her back. 'I'll get her some other way. I'm thinking about it.' Then I laughed. 'Although, I think I've had a pretty good revenge just watching her squirm when Hammond shouted, "I think we've found our Sandy!" and the whole place went wild!'

Erin glared at me and walked on. We all giggled, all except Wizzie.

'Lighten up, Wizzie,' I said. 'What's wrong with you lately?'

'Is that what you really want . . . to get your own back on Erin?'

'What's wrong with that? You do it all the time. Revenge.'

'Her pal didn't get a part in a show. You call that revenge? I'm beginning to think I'm too grown up for you lot.' She was angry, but she was angry at me.

'And what would you call revenge?'

'Something a bit better than that.'

'When you come up with something let me know. And I'll decide what I think about it.'

Wizzie's face went red with rage. 'You'll decide?

You're only in this gang five minutes and you think you make the decisions! Not for me you don't.'

I had taken over from Wizzie, everyone seemed to think that, and Wizzie wasn't happy about that at all. But I had meant to make her laugh, not shout at me. 'Lighten up, Wizzie,' I said again.

'Yeah, Wizzie. It was a joke,' Sonya said.

Wizzie turned on her too. 'What's happened to you lot? You stick up for her! You back her up. You do what she wants. She's changing us!'

'No, she's not,' Grace said. 'We're still the Hell Cats, Wizzie.'

'The Hell Cats? More like the Pussy Cats now.' Wizzie's little face was tight with anger. 'Maybe it's me that's changing then. Maybe I'm just a bit too cool for you lot.' She turned back to me angrily. 'You want revenge? I'll show you what getting your own back on Erin Brodie is.'

CHAPTER FIFTY

Did I hear the siren that night? I imagine now that I did – that it wailed in and out of my dreams. Mum told me next morning at breakfast that she had heard it during the night, but it was when I got to school that I knew the worst.

Rose came flying at me like a wild woman. Running out of the school gates and down the road towards me, screaming. At first, I thought she was heading for someone behind me. I even looked round, and by the time I looked back she was on me, grabbing me by the lapels of my blazer, shaking me. 'You'd g-get her. You said that. You'd g-get her!'

She was sobbing so hard she could hardly get the words out. Stuttering like Sonya.

'What are you talking about?' I asked.

I glanced toward the school gates. Heather stood there, crying her eyes out, being comforted by some other girls. What was happening?

'I could kill you!' Suddenly, Rose butted me so hard I fell back. It hurt her as much as it did me for she stumbled too. The blow made me feel sick.

'What's happened? I don't understand.'

'Don't pretend you don't know!' There were people around her now, holding her back from leaping at me again.

'She's not worth it,' someone said. I looked round them all. They were staring at me with disgust in their eyes.

I looked around for my mates, but none of them were there. This lot looked as if they were ready to thump me. Mrs Tasker came pushing her way through the crowd. She looked disgusted with me too. 'Come with me, Hannah Driscoll.'

She called me by my full name. I really was in trouble. They broke a path for me, stepping away from me, as if they might catch something if they came too close. Someone spat at me and it hit my blazer. Mrs Tasker didn't even notice, wouldn't have cared if she had.

'You're for it this time, Driscoll,' I heard someone else say.

I hurried after the teacher, as much for protection as anything else. 'What is going on, Mrs Tasker?'

She didn't look back. All she said was, 'I really hope you don't know, Hannah.'

Wizzie, Grace and Sonya were already in the head's office when I went in. 'What's all this about?' I asked.

Sonya shrugged. 'We've n-n-not been t-t-old yet.' Nerves bringing on her stutter.

Mr McGinty yelled at us. 'Shut up! Be thankful I'm speaking to you before the police come.'

The police? I glanced at Wizzie. She shrugged too, in that couldn't-care-less fashion that annoyed everyone so much. But she had two little red spots on her white cheeks and I knew she was nervous too.

When the head spoke again, it was me he looked at, me he spoke to. 'There was a fire at Erin Brodie's house last night.'

'What's that got to do with us?' I blurted the words out. I was frightened suddenly. The sirens in the night, had they been heading for Erin's house?

His eyes flashed with anger. 'Don't you dare interrupt me! It would seem it has a lot to do with you. That fire was no accident. It was started deliberately. Rags soaked in petrol were lit and then pushed through her letterbox. A gang of girls was seen running away.'

'Was anybody hurt?' Grace asked nervously.

'It was only sheer luck that there were no serious casualties. Everyone was treated for smoke inhalation and one of the neighbours had to jump from an upstairs window.'

'We weren't that gang of girls,' I snapped out.

'Weren't you?'

Couldn't he see that by the look on our faces? Sonya was ready to burst into tears. Grace was shaking. Wizzie was staring at the floor. Why did she always have to pretend she didn't care?! She refused to look up at him.

'Your parents have been sent for. They'll be here shortly.' I could hear Grace begin to cry now. 'Because of Lauren's mother's disability, the police have gone there.' I had wondered why Lauren wasn't here. I knew now. He looked around us in disgust. 'Get them out of my sight, Mrs Tasker.'

We were herded into an empty room while we waited for our parents and the police to arrive. 'Who could have done this?' I said.

'None of us,' Grace said.

And Wizzie didn't say a word. She sat away from us, with her back turned.

'Any ideas, Wizzie?' I asked.

'How should I know?' she said, her face still turned away from us. I wanted her to look me in the eye and say it.

We sat in silence while we waited. Grace was scared of her dad's reaction. Sonya was crying softly.

Everyone seemed to believe we were guilty. Guilty until proven innocent. Yet there was no real proof against us, was there? A gang of girls seen running away. The town was full of gangs of girls. Could have been any of them. But who?

I knew I didn't do it.

And not the Hell Cats either. There had been a time when I would have believed them capable of anything. That was before I had got to know them, to like them. I had changed my opinion of them entirely. Lauren was too happy rehearsing for the part . . . she wouldn't risk that now. Sonya never thought up anything bad to do. She thought joyriding was the most exciting thing she'd ever done. Grace just followed along behind, did what the rest suggested. Never came up with an idea of her own.

But Wizzie? I tried to believe Wizzie couldn't be capable of this either. Wizzie, who seemed to have a secret life somewhere away from us.

I kept thinking of what she'd said just yesterday and it frightened me.

I'll show you what getting your own back on Erin Brodie is.

Was that what she'd done – shown me what revenge is really like?

CHAPTER FIFTY-ONE

I was proud of my mum for the first time. When the police questioned us, she didn't fall apart as I expected her to. She didn't start screaming and shouting like Grace's dad, or swearing like Sonya's parents. She simply told the police her daughter would never do anything like that, no matter how badly she'd been treated, or how much she resented Erin. I could see she was ready for a good cry, but she held it in. She stuck up for me.

The WPC who was there wouldn't let it go. She started right into me. 'We know there was bad feeling between you girls. They threw you out of their gang. You wanted to get back at Erin.'

I looked at her defiantly. 'They didn't throw me out,' I said. 'I left.'

'They treated her really badly,' Mum said. 'Especially that Erin. Hannah went into a terrible depression. But she pulled herself out of it.' Mum clutched at my hand on my lap. 'I was really proud of the way she pulled herself out of it. And I know she would never do anything to hurt anybody.'

The policewoman didn't look convinced. 'I'd take her down to the police station right now, have her charged.'

She said it as if I was dirt beneath her feet.

'Oh, come on, WPC Duff. She's only a young girl. Let's give her the benefit of the doubt.' The other cop was a man. He even managed a smile at me.

Did they think they were fooling me? I'd seen too many TV cop shows to be taken in by this 'good cop–bad cop' routine.

'Just tell us the truth,' the policeman said.

And what was the truth? Yes. I wanted back at Erin, revenge for all the things she'd done to me. But not like this. 'I don't know anything about that fire,' I said. 'I would never have done anything like that.'

'Maybe your friends did it behind your back.' Bad cop this time.

I shook my head. 'No. We would challenge them to a fight, but we would never do anything like this.'

'You can speak for all your friends, can you?'

I hesitated a moment too long. I knew it sounded like a lie. 'Of course I can.'

Even as I said it I was wondering if it was the truth. How well did I know Wizzie? And I was scared. Scared that she was behind it all.

Wizzie's parents didn't even appear at the school. They had already consulted their solicitor and Wizzie was taken home to be questioned there.

It was Wizzie my mum blamed. 'She's a bad lot. You should keep away from her. I've always told you that. I mean, her family's even got their own solicitor. That tells you how often they're in trouble.'

'But I've never seen any real badness in her, Mum.'

'But you think she might have done this. I can see it in your face.'

And that was what I was really afraid of. The others all felt the same.

We all phoned each other later that night, all except Wizzie. I tried her, we all did, but her phone was switched off as usual.

'We'll all get the blame if they prove it was Wizzie,' Grace said. 'I got a real hiding and it wasn't even me. How can we prove we weren't with her?'

Lauren managed to make us laugh. 'When the police

came to my house my mum kept telling them she would have heard me if I'd got up in the middle of the night to go out and start a fire. She was using sign language at the time. It was so obvious that she wouldn't have heard a bomb going off. Even the cops laughed.'

But all I could think about was Wizzie. 'We have to talk to her,' I said. 'We have to get the truth out of her.'

Next day I half expected Wizzie not to be at school. But she was. Leaning against the gates, looking nonchalant – a good word to describe Wizzie – nonchalant. As if she hadn't a care in the world.

'What happened to you last night? Couldn't get you on the phone.'

'Tired. Decided to have an early night.'

Grace asked the question we all wanted to ask. 'You wouldn't have done this without telling us, would you?'

'You mean, like setting fire to Erin's flat?' She looked all around us, saw in our faces that maybe we did think that. 'Let me ask you something. Did you lot do it without telling me?'

'Of course we didn't.'

'Well, if I can believe you, you can believe me.' Wizzie glared round us all.

Lauren said, 'You're right, Wizzie. Sorry I asked.'

'That's good enough for me.' Sonya said.

But it wasn't good enough for any of us really. Later, when Wizzie was in the toilet, we all shared the same thought. She didn't actually say she hadn't done it.

CHAPTER FIFTY-TWO

The police might not have any proof against us, but that didn't matter at school. We were guilty and they all made sure we knew it. If we hadn't been together I wouldn't even have come to school.

We walked into the canteen, arm in arm. Heads high, we had nothing to be ashamed of. 'You're supposed to be innocent till proved guilty!' I shouted at all the accusing faces.

'In your case we'll make an exception,' someone called back.

Here I was, once again, being blamed for something I didn't do. But this time, at least, I had my friends with me, and they knew I wasn't guilty.

We were left alone. When we walked in somewhere, everyone else walked out.

'Good!' Wizzie yelled after them as they all stomped out of the toilets. 'Prefer privacy anyway!'

She laughed, and was annoyed because none of us joined in. 'Come on, you're always telling me to lighten up . . . Well, I have.'

'Lighten up, Wizzie? This is serious! Nothing to joke about.'

'Nobody got hurt. Wasnae that bad.'

I couldn't believe she'd said that. 'Nobody got hurt? Wizzie, Erin's living in a hostel. Her family have lost everything. They had a lovely house, lovely things.' I remembered how proud Erin's mother had been of her house. The ornate cornices on the ceiling, the beautiful marble tiles in the close. How the living-room wall was dominated by photos of the family she was so proud of. All gone now. The thought of it suddenly made me feel sick.

'Material things. Don't matter. They'll be insured anyway.'

Why was she saying these things? I felt like I didn't know Wizzie at all. 'Is that why you did it?' I had to say it. She drew her eyes up to mine.

'What did you say?'

'She said, "Is that why you did it, Wizzie?"' Lauren stood beside me.

'Just because your family knows every insurance scam in the world, doesn't mean everybody else does.' I couldn't believe Sonya dared to say that to Wizzie.

Neither could Wizzie. She turned on us all. 'I'm telling you I had nothing to do with that fire.'

'Are you sure?'

'I'm sure.' But there was something in her face, in the way she said it. She looked guilty. She sounded guilty. I didn't believe her. I was sure none of the others did either.

No one said a word.

'Do none of you believe me?'

I was the only one who stared right back at her. 'I don't think we do, Wizzie.'

She kicked at the sink. 'Doesn't matter what I say. You don't believe me. Some mates you are.' Her voice was breaking she was so angry. 'Who cares? Who needs you lot? I'm way past you anyway. I'll get better mates than you.'

And she stormed out of the toilets.

Lauren began to cry softly. 'I can't believe she just said that. Not Wizzie.'

Sonya cried. 'My mum says I've to keep back from Wizzie from now on.'

'My dad'll kill me if I run about with her again,' Grace said.

We all thought it had been Wizzie, running with another gang. So why was I the one who felt guilty? Because she did it for me. That was why. I'd wanted revenge. Wizzie got it for me.

It was a day I would never forget. There was disgust for us in everyone's eyes. We couldn't be suspended because there was no real proof against us, but the pupils didn't need proof. They had tried and sentenced us all. The whole school had taken Erin's side and I couldn't blame them.

Wizzie was the only one who didn't seem to care. After that incident in the toilets she ignored us. She acted as if she enjoyed the glares and the comments. She just glared right back at them. But there was anger in her too. I'd never seen such anger. Anger at us, her mates. Because we didn't believe her. But how could we? She was hiding something, and we all knew it.

There was something else too that really bothered me. I could read it in their eyes as they watched Wizzie warily. Now people really were scared of her.

Because if Wizzie could do this . . . what else could she do?

CHAPTER FIFTY-THREE

I walked home alone that day. Lauren went off to rehearsals though she didn't want to. But big Anil came and called for her and he walked with her to the auditorium. 'At least someone doesn't think we're guilty,' Sonya said.

For once, Grace hit the nail on the head. 'No, he doesn't think Lauren's guilty.'

But then, I don't think a lot of people did think Lauren had anything to do with it. Since she'd started rehearsals for the school show she was different. She looked different. She wasn't one of us any more. Everything was changing.

When school finished, I trudged round the corner towards my tenement, and there, standing at the mouth of my close, was Heather. I glanced around, sure Erin and Rose would be somewhere nearby, ready to pounce.

'I'm on my own,' Heather said, her voice trembling.

In fact, she was trembling all over. I thought it was with anger until I came closer and saw the tears in her eyes. Big fat tears. And I knew then it wasn't anger I heard in her voice. It was fear.

Fear? What was Heather afraid of? Me?

'What are you here for?' I asked her.

When she spoke, her voice was a sob. 'I've got something to tell you.' She was crying now, talking through her sobs. 'I didn't mean for all this to happen. I'm so sorry, Hannah.' She took a deep breath before she spoke again. 'It was me,' she said.

'It was you?' What was she talking about? Then, it was as if my brain exploded. She was talking about the fire! Heather had started the fire at Erin's!

The tears were tumbling down her face.

'You set fire to Erin's house?' I asked.

She drew in a great sob and shook her head violently. 'No, no. Of course not that. I didn't do that.'

'What then?'

And even before she spoke I suddenly knew what she was going to say.

'I was the one who told everybody about Erin.'

It was as if the world stopped dead. Erin's secret. It had been Heather all along.

Her words spilled out. 'I heard you that night at the wedding, I saw you going into the ladies with Erin. Followed you. I was so jealous.' Her words came in the middle of her sobs. 'I stood outside, heard you whispering. Best friends, you were saying . . . and I wanted Erin to be my best friend. She told me I was her best friend.' She said that as if it justified everything. 'And I was so annoyed at her. When I heard what she said about me, talking about me as if I was stupid. Not as smart as you and her!'

I remembered that too. Erin, always ready to say something negative about someone.

'I only told one person, just to get it off my chest. I thought I could trust them . . . and then before I knew it, it was all over the school, and Erin blamed you.' She looked at me and sobbed again. 'I was going to tell her it was me, honest, but I thought I'll let you get the blame, serve you right . . . I was just going to let you stew for a while . . . and then, suddenly I was Erin's best friend again. She hated you. I still would have told the truth. I know I would have, Hannah . . . but when I saw how bad they were making things for you – you were out the gang, nobody would talk to you – I was too scared to say it was me. They might do that to me as well.' She drew in a long sob. 'I didn't know it would get as bad as it did.'

I stood there, couldn't move, remembering the pain and the humiliation of those horrible days, weeks. All because of Heather. My heart was thumping. 'You could have stuck up for me, Heather. You knew it wasn't me and you didn't back me up. Just one person believing me would have made all the difference.'

'I was going to. Honest. But . . .' She could hardly speak for crying. 'I was jealous of you. You were funny and everybody wanted to be your mate and you were stealing Erin away from me. I know it was a horrible thing to do, but how was I to know it would get that bad? Then you seemed to be all right. You joined the Hell Cats. And they're really tough. You changed, Hannah. You got just like them. And I didn't care any more.' She stopped for breath. 'But I didn't think you would hate Erin so much you could do this.'

I made a sudden angry rush at her and grabbed her by the collar of her jacket, pushed her up against the wall. Her eyes went wide with fear, frightened of what I might do next. 'I never did anything to Erin. I had nothing to do with that fire. None of us did.' And even as I said it I was thinking . . . *except Wizzie*.

'You said you were going to get us all back,' Heather said. 'Rose didn't get the part in the musical. That really broke her up. You said Erin was next . . . and you set fire to Erin's house.'

'I'm telling you, we didn't.'

I let her go and she crumpled against the wall. 'I know it's my turn next. I was sure you'd found out it was me all the time. You were just waiting your chance to get me. Keeping the worst till last. And I've been so scared. Because if you could do that to get back at Erin . . . what were you going to do to me?'

She was afraid of me. I could see it in her eyes. Heather, who had been my friend for so long, was terrified of me. I didn't like the feeling. I took a step back from her. She had caused all this. I should hate her. I should want to thump the living daylights out of her. A few days ago I probably would have. But not now. I'd had enough of revenge.

'I'm not going to do anything to you, Heather. But I want you to take a message back to Erin. Will you do that for me, Heather?' She nodded. 'I want you to tell her that we had nothing to do with that fire. The Hell Cats are just like us, Heather. Just like the Lip Gloss Girls.' (*All except Wizzie*. The words flitted into my mind, I couldn't stop them.) 'Tell her I'm so sorry it happened. We all are . . . And tell her the truth. Tell her it was because of you everybody found out her secret. Not me. Tell her everything. Will you do that, Heather?'

'I will, Hannah. I promise.'

'On your honour? Because I will come and get you if you don't tell her you were to blame.'

Even as I said it I knew it wasn't the truth. I wouldn't come and get her.

'On my honour.' And she sobbed again, 'I am so sorry, Hannah.'

She sagged with relief. Confession is good for the soul – hadn't I heard that somewhere? Heather's chin was trembling with the crying. I could feel my eyes filling up too. I should hate her. Instead, I felt sorry for her.

'I'm going to Erin, right now.' Heather began to hurry away from me. 'I promise you I'm going to make everything all right.' I watched her as she stumbled away and I wondered if tomorrow she'd behave any differently. Would things have changed?

CHAPTER FIFTY-FOUR

The house was empty when I went inside. Mum was on a late shift. I had no one to talk to – didn't want to talk to anyone anyway. Except perhaps Lauren. But she would still be at rehearsals. I couldn't take it all in. Heather had caused all this. *Heather*. Too afraid to speak out and tell the truth. Too afraid to stick up for me.

And all of a sudden, I was in tears. I would never have cried in front of Heather. Now, I couldn't stop myself. I cried thinking of the shame and hurt I had felt all that time. What Heather had done to me had changed my life. It had all been her fault. I remembered how she'd been right outside the toilets that night at the wedding, waiting to drag us on to the floor for the last dance. I remembered too her annoyance because I had been to Erin's house on my own the very next night. Why hadn't I suspected her before?

Because I'd trusted her.

I wouldn't have thought she was capable of such a thing. Yet she couldn't even stick up for me. She wouldn't even have had to admit that she was the guilty one. All she would have had to do was tell Erin, tell everybody, she believed me.

But, instead, Heather had turned against me, just like Erin and Rose.

All those horrible days and weeks – if just one person had believed me it would have made all the difference.

And it had all led to this. The fire at Erin's and . . . Wizzie.

'I want to believe Wizzie had nothing to do with it.' I said it aloud. Wanted to believe it so much. Because if she wasn't guilty, then I wasn't guilty either.

But she was hiding something. She must have had something to do with it.

Everyone thought Wizzie was trouble. Why should I believe her?

A voice inside answered me. *If just one person had believed me, it would have made all the difference.*

Wizzie had told us she had nothing to do with the fire. She had promised it. None of us had believed her.

Maybe this time, I was the one who could make the

difference.

I was going to believe Wizzie, stand by her. That's what friends did. Maybe that was all Wizzie needed. I didn't want Wizzie to end up feeling the way I had. I was going to do something about it.

Mum had left a note telling me she wanted me to stay home. I didn't want to defy her, not tonight, but I would have to. Because I had to see Wizzie.

I tried to get her on the mobile but it had been switched off again. But I had to talk to her tonight. I couldn't wait until tomorrow. I kept thinking of the night when I was at my lowest. What if Wizzie felt like that tonight? I couldn't take any risks.

Tomorrow might be too late.

CHAPTER FIFTY-FIVE

I took the train to the estate where the Hell Cats lived. Wizzie's area was beyond where the rest of the girls' houses were. Beyond the neat gardens of Lauren's street and out on to the back of beyond. It was scary walking here. If you've never walked through one of those estates, pray you never have to. How could she live here? No wonder Wizzie was hard. You would have to be tough to survive here. And thinking of how tough she was, I wondered if I was just being stupid. Wizzie could face up to anything. Why was I so afraid for her?

The houses on her street looked almost derelict, windows boarded up with steel, and graffiti daubed on walls. There was litter everywhere and gangs of youths were hanging around the street corners. Downtown Baghdad had nothing on this.

'Looking for somebody, hen?' A boy, his hand curled

round a beer can, asked me as I passed him at a street corner.

'Wizzie McLeod,' I gulped.

He pointed the beer can to a block of flats. 'Wee Wizzie? She lives over there. Are you her mate?'

I didn't even know how to answer that. Was I her mate?

I was about to cross the street, when he added, 'But she's no' there. Saw her heading for the chippie.' He pointed the beer can down another street.

All I had to do to find the chippie was follow the smell.

I turned the corner and there was Wizzie, but she wasn't alone. A gang of older girls were crowding round her. The Black Widows. They were easily recognisable, all in black, viciousness written all over them. Wizzie was trying to stand tall, but there was something in the way she was looking up at them that made me realise she was afraid.

Wizzie, afraid?

I slipped into a doorway and listened.

'You know I won't say a word,' she was saying. There was a nervous catch in her voice. 'But you shouldnae have done it. My mates are getting the blame. I'm getting the blame.'

I held my breath.

'You know better than to say anything.' The voice that answered her was threatening. 'You know what happens to grasses, Wizzie.'

Another voice, high-pitched and nasal came in. 'You practically asked us to do it anyway.'

Something of her old boldness burst out of Wizzie. 'I did not! I only told you we were going to get Erin Brodie back. But not like that!'

I peeked round and saw one of the girls grip Wizzie by the shoulder and drag her round the corner. Suddenly they had all gone. I slipped from the doorway and followed them.

Nasal voice was speaking again. 'Well, we showed you what the big girls do when they want to get their own back on somebody, didn't we?'

'I cannae let my mates get the blame for this!' Wizzie sounded as if she was ready to cry. Didn't sound like Wizzie at all.

The harsh threatening voice spoke again. 'I'm telling you, Wizzie, you grass on us and you'll be sorry.'

I'd heard enough. I ran round the corner. They were all surrounding Wizzie. One of them still had her by the shoulder. They were harder than Wizzie, wilder than she could ever be. 'Get your hands off my mate!' I screamed.

With that I yanked at Wizzie, pulling her towards me.

Even Wizzie looked astonished.

The tallest of them turned on me. Her hair was spiked like Wizzie's. Was that who Wizzie had tried to copy, so she could look as tough as that? Close up, this was the ugliest bunch of females I had ever seen. The Hell Cats had nothing in the fierce stakes next to them. 'You keep out of this, hen.' There was a sudden flash of steel as she produced a blade. 'Or I'll give you an extra mouth.'

I gulped when I saw the knife. Why did I always have to be so brave? So stupid. I froze to the spot. Wizzie grabbed at me. 'Run!'

I was after her in a second. The one with the knife caught at my jacket, but I yanked myself free. She hardly held me back a moment. We were off. But they were after us. We raced from the back of the chippie and into the street. Wizzie pulled me round a corner, and I followed her. We tore down a side road, heard them pounding after us. 'Where are we going?' I asked breathlessly.

Wizzie didn't tell me. 'Come on!' She pulled me on. Up back stairs, round back greens, through closes. It seemed to me we were running round in circles. Yet as I ran, everything was becoming clearer. They'd started the fire at Erin's. The Black Widows. Wizzie knew, knew all along, and couldn't tell. Because nobody grasses up here. All the time I could hear them running behind us, catching up. Getting closer every second.

We stopped for breath behind some shops. 'Have we lost them?'

'Not yet,' Wizzie said. And we were off again.

We ran though alleys full of bins and rubbish, broken bits of furniture and boxes. Leaping over them, tripping over them. 'Where are we going?' I asked again.

I don't think Wizzie knew. She was just running, anywhere to get away.

Behind a block of boarded-up flats I had to stop. 'Can't go on.' I sank to the ground.

Wizzie pulled me up. 'Got to,' she said.

I could hear them coming – hear their shouts, their feet splashing through puddles.

Wizzie looked around. There was a shed nearby where the rubbish bins were stored. A slip lock on the door. 'In here,' she said. She was breathless too.

She pulled the lock across, opened the door and helped me inside.

The smell was awful, big green bins overflowing with rubbish. We stepped on broken eggs and Chinese take-aways and heaven knows what else. Wizzie slid the lock back quietly and pulled me right to the back with her. We squeezed ourselves behind the bins, out of sight.

She put her fingers to her lips. 'Sssh,' she said softly.

I could hear them running, their feet pounding closer. I tried not to breathe, too afraid to breathe. Kept picturing the knife in the girl's hand. Their angry shouts were practically outside the shed now. They were swearing, calling us every name they could think of.

They stopped. I could picture them looking round, wondering which way to run next.

Just keep quiet, I thought. *In a minute they'll move on.* I prayed for them to move on.

And that's when I heard the scuttling sound.

It was coming from above my head, from inside one of the overflowing bins. Wizzie heard it too. We looked at each other. Her eyes were wide.

I looked up.

And there at the top of a bin, staring down at me, nose twitching, was a rat.

CHAPTER FIFTY-SIX

I've never known fear like it. Never been that close to a rat. It was huge and ugly with razor-sharp teeth, and it was watching me. I began to shake. I thought for a minute I was going to faint. I wanted to scream, but one cry would alert the Black Widows. I didn't know what was terrifying me more. The rats outside, or the rat inside.

More than one.

I suddenly saw the tip of a nose appear above one of the other bins. I gripped Wizzie's hand. She saw it too. She squeezed back. She was trembling.

I imagined one jumping on my head, and tried to stop from screaming. 'Wizzie . . .' I said it through gritted teeth. Too afraid to open my mouth in case one of them leapt inside. *No! Don't think like that!*

Please, God, I prayed, *let them move on. Please . . .*

'Hey, what about here?' Nasal voice was heading for the shed.

One of the others laughed. 'Bet we've got them. Bet that's where they are.'

She tugged at the door. It sprung open.

Streetlight flooded in. Rats erupted from the bins, looking for a way out – not one rat, not two, but loads of them, legions of them.

The Black Widows screamed.

'Rats!'

'Rats!'

And they ran, with an army of rats at their heels.

It was over in a moment. One minute they were there, the next they were gone, their screams echoing through the night air – and we were forgotten, by the rats and by the Black Widows.

Wizzie and I ran from the shed, still holding hands.

Out in the open air – in the clear moonlight, I went crazy brushing myself down, expecting any minute for a rat to creep from my pocket, land on my hair.

Wizzie was the same, slapping herself frantically as if the rats were climbing all over her.

'I hate this place!' she screamed. 'I hate it.'

Was Wizzie crying? I was almost sure she was.

We ran, hardly knowing where we were running.

Anywhere to get away from the rats. Finally, we stopped at a bus shelter.

'I never thought I'd be grateful for rats,' Wizzie said.

I was still shaking, didn't want to think about that. 'They started the fire, didn't they? The Black Widows. I heard them tell you.'

'I was angry at you. It was my fault, Hannah, bragging about how you didn't know how to get revenge. I was always trying to show off to them. They said, "We'll show you how to get revenge, honey." That's what they called me, "honey", as if they were fond of me.' She shrugged her shoulders. 'I didn't expect them to do that. They even bragged to me about it. I tried to tell them, I couldn't let my mates take the blame. But you heard them. If I opened my mouth I'd be for it.' Wizzie was breathless, stopped for a moment. 'I thought they were my mates as well. I thought I wanted to be like them. But I couldn't have done anything like that, Hannah.'

'You could never be like them, Wizzie. They *are* scum of the earth, and you're decent.'

Wizzie let out a long sigh. In the streetlight I saw her scars. 'Did they do that?' I asked. I was suddenly sure I knew where Wizzie's scars had come from.